AFRICAN WRITERS SERIES   FOUNDING EDITOR   Chinua Achebe

PETER ABRAHAMS
6 *Mine Boy*

CHINUA ACHEBE
1 *Things Fall Apart*
3 *No Longer at Ease*
16 *Arrow of God*
31 *A Man of the People*
100 *Girls at War**
120 *Beware Soul Brother†*

THOMAS AKARE
241 *The Slums*

TEWFIK AL-HAKIM
117 *The Fate of a Cockroach‡*

T. M. ALUKO
11 *One Man, One Matchet*
30 *One Man, One Wife*
32 *Kinsman and Foreman*
70 *Chief, the Honourable Minister*
130 *His Worshipful Majesty*
142 *Wrong Ones in the Dock*

ELECHI AMADI
25 *The Concubine*
44 *The Great Ponds*
140 *Sunset in Biafra§*
210 *The Slave*

JARED ANGIRA
111 *Silent Voices†*

I. N. C. ANIEBO
148 *The Anonymity of Sacrifice*
206 *The Journey Within*

AYI KWEI ARMAH
43 *The Beautyful Ones Are Not Yet Born*
154 *Fragments*
155 *Why Are We So Blest?*
194 *The Healers*
218 *Two Thousand Seasons*

BEDIAKO ASARE
59 *Rebel*

KOFI AWOONOR
108 *This Earth, My Brother*

MARIAMA BÂ
248 *So Long a Letter*

FRANCIS BEBEY
205 *The Ashanti Doll*

MONGO BETI
13 *Mission to Kala*
77 *King Lazarus*
88 *The Poor Christ of Bomba*
181 *Perpetua and the Habit of Unhappiness*
214 *Remember Ruben*

STEVE BIKO
217 *I Write What I like§*

OKOT P'BITEK
147 *The Horn of My Love†*
193 *Hare and Hornbill**

YAW M. BOATENG
186 *The Return*

DENNIS BRUTUS
46 *Letters to Martha†*
115 *A Simple Lust†*
208 *Stubborn Hope†*

AMILCAR CABRAL
198 *Unity and Struggle§*

SYL CHENEY-COKER
221 *The Graveyard Also Has Teeth†*

Novels are unmarked
*Short Stories
†Poetry
‡Plays
§Biography/Politics

DRISS CHRAIBI
79 *Heirs to the Past*

J. P. CLARK
50 *America, Their America§*

WILLIAM CONTON
12 *The African*

BERNARD B. DADIE
87 *Climbié*

DANIACHEW WORKU
125 *The Thirteenth Sun*

MODIKWE DIKOBE
124 *The Marabi Dance*

DAVID DIOP
174 *Hammer Blows†*

MBELLA SONNE DIPOKO
57 *Because of Women*
82 *A Few Nights and Days*
107 *Black and White in Love†*

AMU DJOLETO
41 *The Strange Man*
161 *Money Galore*

T. OBINKARAM ECHEWA
168 *The Land's Lord*
245 *The Crippled Dancer*

CYPRIAN EKWENSI
2 *Burning Grass*
5 *People of the City*
19 *Lokotown**
84 *Beautiful Feathers*
146 *Jagua Nana*
172 *Restless City**
185 *Survive the Peace*

BUCHI EMECHETA
227 *The Joys of Motherhood*

OLAUDAH EQUIANO
10 *Equiano's Travels§*

MALICK FALL
144 *The Wound*

NURUDDIN FARAH
80 *From a Crooked Rib*
184 *A Naked Needle*
226 *Sweet and Sour Milk*

MUGO GATHERU
20 *Child of Two Worlds§*

FATHY GHANEM
223 *The Man Who Lost His Shadow*

NADINE GORDIMER
177 *Some Monday for Sure**

JOE DE GRAFT
166 *Beneath the Jazz and Brass†*

BESSIE HEAD
101 *Maru*
149 *A Question of Power*
182 *The Collector of Treasures**
220 *Serowe: Village of the Rain Winds§*
247 *When Rain Clouds Gather*

LUIS BERNARDO HONWANA
60 *We Killed Mangy-Dog**

TAHA HUSSEIN
228 *An Egyptian Childhood*

SONALLAH IBRAHIM
95 *The Smell of It**

YUSUF IDRIS
209 *The Cheapest Nights**

OBOTUNDE IJIMÈRE
18 *The Imprisonment of Obatala‡*

EDDIE IROH
189 *Forty-Eight Guns for the General*
213 *Toads of War*

KENJO JUMBAM
231 *The White Man of God*

AUBREY KACHINGWE
24 *No Easy Task*

SAMUEL KAHIGA
158 *The Girl from Abroad*

CHEIKH HAMIDOU KANE
119 *Ambiguous Adventure*

KENNETH KAUNDA
4 *Zambia Shall be Free§*

LEGSON KAYIRA
162 *The Detainee*

A. W. KAYPER-MENSAH
157 *The Drummer in Our Time†*

JOMO KENYATTA
219 *Facing Mount Kenya§*

ASARE KONADU
40 *A Woman in her Prime*
55 *Ordained by the Oracle*

AHMADOU KOUROUMA
239 *The Suns of Independence*

MAZISI KUNENE
211 *Emperor Shaka the Great†*
234 *Anthem of the Decades†*
235 *The Ancestors†*

ALEX LA GUMA
35 *A Walk in [...]*
110 *In the Fo[...]*
152 *The Sto[...]*
212 *Time of [...]*

DORIS LESS[...]
131 *The Gr[...]*

TABAN LO [...]
69 *Fixion[...]*
74 *Eating [...]*
90 *Franta [...]*
Ribs†
116 *Anot[...]*

BONNIE [...]
105 *The [...]*

YULISA [...]
89 *Oba [...]*
137 *No [...]*
Futu[...]

NAGUI[...]
151 *Mi[...]*
197 *Mi[...]*
225 *Children of Gebela[...]*

NELSON MANDELA
123 *No Easy Walk to Freedom§*

JACK MAPANJE
236 *Of Chameleons and Gods†*

RENE MARAN
135 *Batouala*
DAMBUDZO MARECHERA
207 *The House of Hunger**
237 *Black Sunlight*
ALI A. MAZRUI
97 *The Trial of Christopher Okigbo*
TOM MBOYA
81 *The Challenge of Nationhood (Speeches)* §
S. O. MEZU
113 *Behind the Rising Sun*
THOMAS MOFOLO
229 *Chaka*
HAM MUKASA
133 *Sir Apolo Kagwa Discovers Britain* §
DOMINIC MULAISHO
98 *The Tongue of the Dumb*
204 *The Smoke that Thunders*
CHARLES L. MUNGOSHI
170 *Waiting for the Rain*
JOHN MUNOYNE
21 *The Only Son*
45 *Obi*
94 *Oil Man of Obange*
153 *A Dancer of Fortune*
195 *Bridge to a Wedding*
MARTHA MVUNGI
159 *Three Solid Stones**
MEJA MWANGI
143 *Kill Me Quick*
145 *Carcase for Hounds*
176 *Going Down River Road*
GEORGE SIMEON MWASE
160 *Strike a Blow and Die* §
NGUGI WA THIONG'O
7 *Weep Not, Child*
17 *The River Between*
36 *A Grain of Wheat*
51 *The Black Hermit* ‡
150 *Secret Lives**
188 *Petals of Blood*
200 *Devil on the Cross*
240 *Detained* §
246 *Ngaahika Ndeenda* ‡
NGUGI & MICERE MUGO
191 *The Trial of Dedan Kimathi* ‡
REBEKA NJAU
203 *Ripples in the Pool*
ARTHUR NORTJE
141 *Dead Roots* †
NKEM NWANKWO
67 *Danda*
173 *My Mercedes is Bigger Than Yours*
FLORA NWAPA
26 *Efuru*
56 *Idu*
S. NYAMFUKUDZA
233 *The Non-Believer's Journey*
ONUORA NZEKWU
85 *Wand of Noble Wood*
91 *Blade Among the Boys*
OLUSEGUN OBASANJO
249 *My Command* §
OGINGA ODINGA
38 *Not Yet Uhuru* §

GABRIEL OKARA
68 *The Voice*
183 *The Fisherman's Invocation* †
CHRISTOPHER OKIGBO
62 *Labyrinths* †
KOLE OMOTOSO
102 *The Edifice*
122 *The Combat*
SEMBENE OUSMANE
63 *God's Bits of Wood*
92 *The Money-Order*
175 *Xala*
YAMBO OUOLOGUEM
99 *Bound to Violence*
MARTIN OWUSU
138 *The Sudden Return* ‡
FERDINAND OYONO
29 *Houseboy*
39 *The Old Man and the Medal*
PETER K. PALANGYO
53 *Dying in the Sun*
SOL T. PLAATJE
201 *Mhudi*
R. L. PETENI
178 *Hill of Fools*
LENRIE PETERS
22 *The Second Round*
37 *Satellites* †
238 *Selected Poetry* †
J.-J. RABEARIVELO
167 *Translations from the Night* †
MUKOTANI RUGYENDO
187 *The Barbed Wire & Other Plays* ‡
MWANGI RUHENI
139 *The Future Leaders*
156 *The Minister's Daughter*
TAYEB SALIH
47 *The Wedding of Zein**
66 *Season of Migration to the North*
STANLAKE SAMKANGE
33 *On Trial for my Country*
169 *The Mourned One*
190 *Year of the Uprising*
WILLIAMS SASSINE
199 *Wirriyamu*
KOBINA SEKYI
136 *The Blinkards* ‡
SAHLE SELLASSIE
52 *The Afersata*
163 *Warrior King*
FRANCIS SELORMEY
27 *The Narrow Path*
L. S. SENGHOR
71 *Nocturnes* †
180 *Prose and Poetry*
ROBERT SERUMAGA
54 *Return to the Shadows*
WOLE SOYINKA
76 *The Interpreters*
TCHICAYA U TAM'SI
72 *Selected Poems* †
CAN THEMBA
104 *The Will to Die**
REMS NNA UMEASIEGBU
61 *The Way We Lived**
LAWRENCE VAMBE
112 *An Ill-Fated People* §

J. L. VIEIRA
202 *The Real Life of Domingos Xavier*
222 *Luuanda*
JOHN YA-OTTO
244 *Battlefront Namibia* §
ASIEDU YIRENKYI
216 *Kivuli and Other Plays* ‡
D. M. ZWELONKE
128 *Robben Island*
COLLECTIONS OF PROSE
9 *Modern African Prose*
14 *Quartet*
23 *The Origin of Life and Death*
48 *Not Even God is Ripe Enough*
58 *Political Spider*
73 *North African Writing*
75 *Myths and Legends of the Swahili*
83 *Myths and Legends of the Congo*
109 *Onitsha Market Literature*
118 *Amadu's Bundle*
132 *Two Centuries of African English*
192 *Egyptian Short Stories*
243 *Africa South Contemporary Writings*
ANTHOLOGIES OF POETRY
8 *A Book of African Verse*
42 *Messages: Poems from Ghana*
64 *Seven South African Poets*
93 *A Choice of Flowers*
96 *Poems from East Africa*
106 *French African Verse*
129 *Igbo Traditional Verse*
164 *Black Poets in South Africa*
171 *Poems of Black Africa*
192 *Anthology of Swahili Poetry*
215 *Poems from Angola*
230 *Poets to the People*
COLLECTIONS OF PLAYS
28 *Short East African Plays*
34 *Ten One-Act Plays*
78 *Short African Plays*
114 *Five African Plays*
127 *Nine African Plays for Radio*
134 *African Theatre*
165 *African Plays for Playing 1*
179 *African Plays for Playing 2*
224 *South African People's Plays*
232 *Egyptian One-Act Plays*

KING LAZARUS

A NOVEL

by

MONGO BETI

HEINEMANN

LONDON IBADAN NAIROBI

843
B563K

Heinemann Educational Books Ltd
22 Bedford Square, London WC1B 3HH
PMB 5205 Ibadan · POB 45314 Nairobi
EDINBURGH MELBOURNE AUCKLAND
KINGSTON HONG KONG SINGAPORE KUALA LUMPUR
NEW DELHI PORT OF SPAIN
Heinemann Educational Books Inc.
4 Front Street, Exeter, New Hampshire 03833, USA

ISBN 0 435 90077 3

First published in French as
Le Roi Miraculé 1958
© 1958 Editions Buchet – Chastel – Corrêa
This translation © 1960 Frederick Muller Ltd
First published in *African Writers Series* 1970
Reprinted 1971, 1977, 1980, 1982

Made and printed in Great Britain by
Richard Clay (The Chaucer Press) Ltd,
Bungay, Suffolk

INTRODUCTORY NOTE

IN 1948 the Essazam—a large, somewhat primitive community—were scattered over a wide area, beyond modernising influences. At the turn of the century the tribe had been subjected to the formidable discipline of German colonisation, yet had not entirely lost a natural unruliness towards Authority. It was divided into countless small family clans, all struggling jealously to preserve independence. The Essazam maintained themselves in a very frugal way, by hunting, primitive agriculture and a few small herds of starving cattle. They also had one or two scattered cocoa-plantations, from which they wrung a meagre supplementary income.

Both the German administrators and their French successors had always classified the Essazam (with most other Bantu tribes) as "easily manageable". This was because of internal feuds and vendettas, which legend invested with almost superhuman bloody-mindedness. Of these official policy took full advantage. Estimated numbers were over a hundred thousand, individuals, relatively sound in mind and body, despite progressive inroads by V.D., alcoholism, penal servitude, conscription in two World Wars, lure of the Big City and other scourges of modern civilisation.

Though often changing both appearance and site, the village of Essazam was regarded as the tribe's historic birthplace. The Ebazok clan who inhabited it were held to be the original nucleus of growth and prosperity inherited by other clans.

To the best of anyone's recollection, in 1948 there was

only one important matter which stirred the Essazam into conflict with French Administration. At the end of the First World War, after the Germans' eviction, the Essazam had been saddled with a Chief whom they regarded as an interloper—a capricious, authoritarian ex-sergeant-major, without a drop of Essazam blood. Consequently they conducted a long campaign against him, using every known obstructive device, till he was ousted by the legitimate claims of a young man, Essomba Mendouga: direct descendant of that legendary Chief who had reigned during German colonial rule, but had since died.

Thereafter the tribe relapsed into dismal lethargy until the Second World War, which was followed—even in Essazam territory—by anarchy and confusion. These disturbances made the tribe increasingly decadent.

1

As he lowered himself heavily into his chair, he had an odd sensation. At one particular instant, quick as a wink or flutter of an eyelid, everything seemed abruptly to *come alive*, achieving new depth and focus. It happened as his bottom touched the seat, but before he stretched his legs. There was an imperceptible *frisson*, a flash of light, like sun reflected off metal: the incident had no reality, belonging to the past practically before it happened. So minute a break in his normal outlook made it difficult to convince himself he had *really* felt it, that it was responsible for that indefinable, inexpressible something vitalising this particular July afternoon like a charge of electricity, setting it for ever apart from the rest.

Had he been compelled—say on pain of death—to describe this phenomenon, isolating it from his everyday existence, after cudgelling his brain he might have called it a break in natural rhythm. Yet this image would have proved inadequate. What struck him most forcibly afterwards was not any speeding up or slowing down of normal awareness, but rather that this sudden shock (or whatever it was) had the power of breathing life into inanimate objects. It brought everything, so to speak, bolt upright before him, and gave an interrogatory air to the scene. He felt the landscape and its objects somehow become a person with whom he was liable at any time to be confronted. It struck him, examining this radical split of perception, that the difference between his old and new vision was this : stone and metal had acquired life; the dead, stagnant pool had been transformed into a tumbling river.

Instead of the clumsy, shapeless clouds he had expected to contemplate—as he did, day in day out—perplexed, he found himself looking at something quite different. Against a blue background two adolescents, with the fragility peculiar to youth, grey with dust collected tumbling on the ground, slowly, luxuriously, drew apart from a long embrace. What of that saucy breeze, unaffected by gathering stormclouds on the horizon, challenging the sun with refreshing coolness? Was that not the breath of a living person, predictable of intention, taking pleasure in neutralising the sun's grilling heat? Under its caressing touch the nearby palm and coconut trees seemed to bridle like women : nodding heads, bending, straightening again.

He sat stiff and upright outside his house. The chair, with its supporting back, was of yellowed rattan, low to the ground : like the throne of some ascetic king, perched on the top step of the porch, which was unexpectedly transformed into a dais. The porch itself, incompetently designed, had a baroque air. The whole house was one of his proudest possessions : a superior, tropical-style palace. Its dazzling whiteness dominated the surrounding forest tyrannically : against it the foliage looked not green, but sombre and defeated.

Across the knees of his blue cotton trousers lay his fly-whisk, a cane-yellow stripe, one end shock-headed like Struwwelpeter. A short-sleeved khaki shirt, with epaulettes, completed his ordinary undress uniform. His large naked feet, splayed on the concrete, resembled giant Equatorial toads. This afternoon a sticky, gum-like sweat glued them to the ground, leaving tiny, moist patches around the imprints of the Chief's toes. This was unusual. Today the Chief had neglected the shade of the ornamental trees around the porch and come out instead on to the open part of the porch, exposed on all sides to the sun's vertical rays. Instead of consuming him, their fieriness lapped him as tenderly as a tepid early-morning shower—the sort taken in the rainy season, when everything is damp and cool.

With enormous effort he occasionally half-opened his eyes, contemplating the village, *his* village: Essazam. It consisted of two interminable rows of mud-huts, among them the occasional small brick house. The parallel rows were facing, constructed down two sides of a long rectangular village square; straggling to a dead end beside the main road. The view was sketchy. Simplicity offset an intransigence of mood with an equally arresting naïve charm. A stylised picture, that might have been drawn by too clever a schoolboy.

The Chief did not see it so. He had never been to school. To stylise any particular landscape, express it in abstract terms, laying bare basic geometrical patterns, was possible only for someone lacking flesh-and-blood ties with it: a child, tourist, or explorer. The Chief was Essazam bred. His father belonged; his brothers and children too. He could have recited its history with the wealth of detail he employed telling stories to Maurice or Isabelle—at least, to the children they had had before leaving for the big town. God alone knew what they did there.

His village! Down in the middle, a white cube of a house gleamed in the sunlight, its roof a bright sheet of corrugated iron. That was where his first wife, Makrita, lived, the only one Le Guen agreed to baptise. The others also wanted it, but Le Guen said he was not authorised to do them. *Women....*

Among the left-hand row of huts he was astonished to pick out—for the first time in years—a modest, familiar dwelling of adobe and straw. His mother had lived there. A humble, unpretentious woman, refusing to move before death. From this house, on one ill-omened night, the keening cry of the women mourners had announced her end. Until then he had never imagined their separation.

Nearer his own home—next door almost—stood an elegant little house: so new, pretty and delicate in design that it reminded one of a gazelle. To avoid jealousy, this was where his twenty-third wife officially lived. Anaba was young and beautiful, a dewy adolescent type he particularly liked. She spent most of her time under his roof. She had hardly left him since her arrival nearly a year earlier. Now he could hear her moving to and fro above his head, on the only upper floor of the Palace.

Ordinarily he could not consciously have worked this out. The scene flaunted the bright colours which had gone into making up his past. He had neutralised this rich palette into a dull grey monochrome and kept it so. For all its violence and variety of incident, his life lacked one thing. He had never known that special heightening of faculties that illness bestowed.

When he half-opened his eyes to watch the passing lorries jolt along with flapping tarpaulins, they looked different. Their mud-coloured paint made him think of some swamp animal. Their hurry had the harassed air of someone accomplishing a superhuman task. Each lorry resembled a gigantic louse, half frantic in the surrounding red dust.

He also had the sensation of continual movement; felt himself dwindling into the distance, without any fixed point of focus. It was as though a powerful invisible hand dragged him away. Helplessly, in panic, he was wafted off without so much as leaving his porch. Everything cherished slipped from him—even the sun itself. Its brassy glare did not allay the icy chill running through him. He began to shiver.

A kind of surgical operation then took place as rising fever severed him painlessly from the rest of the world. Everything went on apart from him.

Though his actual vision was somewhat blurred, objects assumed that hard prominence one normally sees stamped upon the faces of strangers. He had spent his life in a world of false appearances. The veil between himself and reality had blown away, leaving only wisps behind. The wind of its passage was like a tornado, casting him ashore upon a lonely, unfamiliar island. He was the flotsam of shipwreck.

This illness could be described as one of frustration. It was like being in a lions' den (how many times had he heard the story of the prophet thrown to them?). He was without company.

For a moment he fancied himself shrouded in darkness; a darkness so intense that *he could not find his way back to himself*. His mind and will were dissociated from his physical body. His actions remained either undone or only partially accomplished, in a bungling fashion. His limbs lacked co-ordination. Clumsily he put out one hand and fumbled about for some time before clutching the flywhisk. He could not even raise his knee to bring the wretched object nearer his grasp. He had been robbed of control over his own body.

With an enormous effort he managed briefly to pull himself together. His mind, his limbs, and above all his eyes came into temporary use. Painfully he concentrated his gaze upon the centre of the village—which seemed an enormous distance away. He saw a man coming towards him, but in such a roundabout, leisurely way. He seemed to recognise the dawdling figure. Surely it was his young brother Mekanda? Yes! *But can't he hurry up?* the Chief groaned to himself. A spasm of panic clutched at him. Not that he would have dreamed of shouting for help. He still had to discover the exact nature of the threatening danger. In truth, he was rather enjoying this new experience.

He was on the point of dropping off into a comfortable

sleep when the noisy roar of a motor-bike jerked him awake again. He knew that sound of old. Taking advantage of this unexpected stimulus, he watched Le Guen, the priest, park by the roadside, march into the village with his long, authoritative stride. The Chief swore to himself. Le Guen was following the same queer pattern of movement as Mekanda, popping first into one house, then into that across the road, and so on. The Chief's mind began to wander. He failed to recollect that the missionary's visits had always followed this zig-zag route and Mekanda had not been slow to copy him. The collector of Ebazok taxes, and the man of God sent to convert the Essazam, had much in common, including preoccupation with speed and efficiency. Both were representative of their generation.

At the moment more than half the village separated them, but the white man forged ahead energetically. His jerky, violent strides were inappropriate to his diminutive stature. The Chief wondered if, finally, he would catch up with Mekanda. This private guessing-game, this urge to watch a race to the end, had a restorative effect. Temporarily he shook off the effects of his fever and for a little was brought back to the world.

It was Mekanda who reached him first, carrying an enormous account-book. This he at once opened and began to riffle busily through the pages, grumbling under his breath the whole time—a frequent habit.

"Greetings, O Chief!" he muttered vaguely. This between inaudible asides and without raising his eyes from his ledger.

"Greetings, brother!" the Chief replied, astonished at his verbal feat. At any other time, after fixing his face in a benevolent smile, he would have settled back to listen to his brother's usual indictment of the Ebazok clan's lack of civic responsibility. The Chief sat silent, stiffer than ever, teeth clenched. Mekanda was so busy being indignant that he failed to notice.

"Listen, Chief," he muttered, "they're really laying it on a bit thick this time. Our worthy blood-brothers are *exaggerating* again. Just as they did last year. And the older men, who ought to set a good example, are the worst of the lot. They're repeating the old nonsense about shifting their tax-liability on to *you*. This time we won't make any more concessions, eh, Chief? They've fleeced us enough that way already. Oh, last year they may have had some sort of an excuse. The bottom falling out of the cocoa market; fair enough. But they've made a packet on cocoa these last few months. If you aren't careful, Chief, they'll try to establish last year's concession as a precedent. Supposing the elders in the other clans decide to take the same line? Maybe you ought to deal with them in person, Chief. When I bawl them out, it doesn't work. You go and get really angry, blow your top——"

"What about the small villages?"

"Oh the village people are no trouble. I'm worried about here. They've heard a rumour that those above a certain age-limit are to be excused all taxes. They fancy this provision to be actually in operation. I suppose belonging to the Chief's clan gives them these bright ideas!"

"Who's really behind it all?"

"*Who?*" repeated Mekanda, furiously. "Why, all of them, Chief—practically every single elder!" He waved his ledger about like a schoolboy in a pet. "There's Ezoum, of course—he's paid up regularly for ages; then he's a religious chap, teaches catechism. You can count in the other Christians—there aren't many of them—and that's the lot."

"What about Ondoua?"

"I was just coming to him. For a sheer smooth talker that old devil's unbeatable! He's always telling other people how to behave and what our ancestors would have

15

done in similar circumstances. He's just married off his daughter, too, so he must be rolling in cash. Do you imagine he'll pay up promptly? Not on your life. Nothing but words, words, words. If there's one thing I'd gladly do without, it's my daily call on that bloody liar——"

"Listen, Mekanda, he's an old man. You ought to show proper respect for him."

"Oh, I don't say to his face what I think about him and his lies. That doesn't mean I can't——"

The Chief listened attentively while his young brother continued conversing with—well, whom? Who was it imitated him so well that he had interrupted Mekanda? Addressing him by name, to indicate annoyance, just as the Chief would have done himself? Enough to make him suspect himself of leading a kind of double life or having a spirit to take over from him. He was amazed his brother had not noticed the imposture. Mekanda should have picked the Chief out from his double.

"Let Makrita take care of this business. Tell her, from me, that she's to make herself responsible for it——"

Hardly had he uttered these words in a voice already beginning to quaver alarmingly than Le Guen swept briskly up the steps. He waved a greeting, pulled up a chair, and seated himself down beside the Chief, not opposite him. He yawned vastly two or three times, then asked in a cheerful voice for a glass of cold water, addressing no one in particular. This lack of deference was one of Le Guen's characteristics.

There was certainly a miracle somewhere in this affair. Each person concerned thought it took place at whichever moment most stirred his sensibility. The only true miracle happened when Le Guen sat beside the Chief. Until then immobilised by fever, he suddenly sat up straight, pulled himself completely together. He talked in a firm, clear voice, as if he had, quite literally, come back from the dead.

"Go and fetch the missionary some cold water," he told his brother. "Make sure the glass is spotlessly clean. These people are very delicate; the least bit of dirt is fatal to them."

Mekanda called to the girl, who was still padding about audibly overhead: "Bring some cold water for the missionary. Wipe the glass carefully first. These white folk are so *fragile*, you know!"

Ten years' sojourn among the Essazam had made Le Guen familiar both with them and their customs. Once he had laughed aloud. Now he merely smiled. When he wrote home to his mother about the 1946 Christmas celebrations, it took several pages to tell her how the Saviour had chosen this blessed night to reward the piety of one of his female parishioners. This lady (little Gustave's mother) had given birth to a fine boy. Had the decision been left to her, she would cheerfully have christened the child Jesus. Le Guen, who had practically become a native himself, omitted the one detail which gave his account a picturesque flavour. Since the Essazam have no professional midwives, their womenfolk call in friends and neighbours at the onset of labour. Directly the child is born, they improvise a celebration party. Numerous presents are exchanged. Therefore the missionary's family remained perplexed by this letter. They felt something was missing. They were quite right. Le Guen behaved as though knowledge of the customs were automatically shared by outsiders.

He pulled his topee down over his eyes to protect them from the sun's glare. Absentmindedly he made a little joke. This, too, was part of his routine.

"Well, now, Chief, how goes it? Healthy as ever? Palm-wine, that's the stuff, eh? Drink it when you're sickening, while you're sick and during your convalescence! Isn't that right?"

He finished off this speech with the usual short snort

17

of laughter. The Chief tried to laugh also, but only managed a throttled grunt which hurt him horribly.

The missionary asked his other regular question.

"Chief, people are always saying that you've never had a day's illness in your life. Tell me, is that honestly so?"

"It is so, my son," the Chief said. "That's the honest truth. I've never been ill once."

"How have you managed it, Chief? That's what I'd like to know."

"Cold water," said Mekanda, emerging for a moment from his ledger. He had been buried in columns of figures ever since Le Guen appeared. The priest's visits were notably brief.

Le Guen turned to the younger man, hand outstretched, a chagrined smile upon his face. He looked like a grown-up who has been making a fool of himself in a children's charade. Then he looked behind him. Anaba stood holding a glass of water. To judge by the amused expression on her face, she had been waiting some time. Again they had contrived to pull his leg. Every time they played little jokes upon him. Every time Le Guen allowed himself to be caught.

He gulped down the water at one go and sat waving his glass about. This trick went back to the days when he claimed that the practice enabled him to avoid drinking the sediment at the bottom and consequent infection. He returned the glass, thanked Anaba, breathed heavily for a moment, then said: "Chief, tomorrow—*whoo-o-o-m!*" This onomatopoeic utterance was accompanied by a one-handed gesture suggesting a car hurtling down the road.

"You're going away?" Mekanda asked.

"Indeed, yes. To Ongola. If there's any little errand you'd like me to run, Chief—perhaps a message you'd like delivered? That's really why I dropped in."

The Chief made no reply. Le Guen turned, for the first time that day really looking at him. Something remarkable was happening which took Le Guen so aback that he later believed it to be when the miracle occurred. The Chief's eyes always were somewhat striking: red-veined, dilated, and bulging as if to burst from his head. Now they were glazed by fever. The Chief stared fixedly at the rosaries and scapulars which swung in a bunch from Le Guen's arm. Perhaps the Chief sought to estimate their worth to himself. What revelations would they vouchsafe, if he showed faith in their powers by adopting them while there was time? He might thus have convinced himself that the legendary Akomo was a genuine blood relation. The problem had nagged uncomfortably all his life. Since childhood events had encouraged him to believe in this lordly pedigree. All things pointed in the same direction. He became a reincarnation of a figure who had always seemed very real.

But events during the last few years gave rise to doubt and guilt. He nursed resentment. He had committed many sins during the war for which he still found it hard to forgive himself. In particular, complying with requests to surrender certain members of his tribe for penal servitude. Some never returned. (This had taken place at the time of forced-labour battalions.)

Le Guen picked out whatever element in the complex human soul was likely to justify his priestly function. He would never have thought the Chief not religious by nature. Yet it was so, unless religion included the following qualities. Solicitude to ensure the maximum opportunities in life for himself whilst still preserving supreme power. A violent desire for knowledge—all-embracing knowledge, attainable by various short cuts, bypassing the hard, unending labour required for intellectual effort. Also a readiness to believe the worst always—not from desire but conviction that fate was certain to deal him some nasty knocks. He clung to this certainty, as though its familiarity could act as a prophylactic.

That was how he convinced himself that he was now dying. Without a doubt the bell had tolled for him. The prospect of death held a single consolation. Once and for all he could discover whether or not he really was descended from Akomo. How should such a scion behave during these last moments on earth? What mien was most likely to make his illustrious ancestor proud of him?

Instead of replying to Le Guen, he pointed a trembling forefinger at the bunch of devotional objects hanging from the missionary's arm. Whether the Chief were delirious, making an unaccustomed joke, or had a definite purpose, was uncertain. Le Guen was knocked off his perch. He stammered, became entangled in a long sentence, only to start again. Finally he launched into a spluttering apologia. He explained regretfully to the Chief that all these objects had already been purchased. They no longer belonged to him. He must deliver them to their proper owners. He had been unable to call upon them all during his visit. He expected them to call upon him at the mission-house to claim their purchases.

"You must have *one* left that hasn't been disposed of, Father," Mekanda suggested, demurely. He was in a leg-pulling mood now, enjoying Le Guen's embarrassment.

"No, no, indeed," the missionary protested. "That's really the truth. They're no longer mine to dispose of, not one of them——"

"You surprise me," Mekanda murmured, ironically insistent. "You really astonish me. In the normal way you've always got a stack of second-hand rosaries for re-sale."

"Not this time," Le Guen repeated, more embarrassed than ever by his little lie. "These already belong to somebody. I shall bring back some more from Ongola. I shall then be delighted to make the Chief a present of some of them, if he still wants them."

Le Guen was not to be kept down for long.

20

What other professional proselytiser would have gone to such lengths to avoid a brutal declaration of principle? Anyone else would have replied: *Chief, I cannot deliberately place in your hands a devotional object which has been blessed by a priest. You are not only a pagan, but fundamentally a tainted man. You practise fornication several times every night with various women.* Such a pronouncement would have relieved both Le Guen's conscience and his feelings. Instead, he silently thrashed out a very serious problem. By sticking too faithfully to the letter of the law, was he in danger of committing a far more unpardonable sin of omission? What if he failed to rescue a new and most precious soul for God?

When he rose to go he was still in a dilemma. He waved his usual vague goodbye and hastily plunged down the steps. In a village where no one normally hurried, he resembled the herald of some frightful disaster. With enormous strides he hurried down the whole length of the square. Going back to his machine, he paused several times to mop his face with a handkerchief. The Chief, his brother and young wife, followed Le Guen's departure. A strong wind was getting up: the missionary's white soutane flapped and ballooned round him. The Chief began to lose contact with his surroundings again. He released his grip on consciousness, letting himself go. Faintly he heard the loud reverberations of Le Guen's exhaust-pipe. Like the tom-toms of Akomo's heroic warriors the noise swelled and faded. It paused, but only for a moment. He worked out that Le Guen must be turning off the road on to the track leading to the Catholic Mission. Finally the sound died away abruptly as it had begun. Le Guen had pulled up outside his presbytery.

All that evening he was haunted by the dream which had obsessed him ever since meeting the Chief. On this occasion its form was an imagined scene; a set-piece ravishing the missionary's senses with its exotic colourfulness. All around him soared the Gothic arches of a magnificent cathedral, with a great image of the Crucified Christ spreading out His arms to all humanity. At the foot of the high altar humbly knelt a gigantic African Negro. A pagan, abjuring his heathen past in shame. A black angel draped in the white robe of the Heavenly Elect, ready to burn all he had formerly adored. This neophyte's curly head was bowed beneath the white, slender hands of one of Christ's earthly apostles—a tall young man whose lined, ecstatic features resembled those of Le Guen.

Decidedly an ambiguous vision. Perhaps a fragment of extraordinary symbolism?

To calm his nerves he sat down that same evening to write a long letter to his mother.

You enjoy hearing factual details about this kingdom in which I am a humble citizen, don't you, Mama? Well, since my last letter—you remember, the one in which I told you that your beloved Bantu monarch had just married his twenty-third wife?—there has been nothing noteworthy to report till this afternoon.

I had been calling upon the Christian families in the country villages; making a tour of the district round about the Catholic Mission. About half-past one I was on my way back still carrying one or two rosaries and scapulars hung upon my left arm—remains of the supply with which I'd started out. As I passed by along the main road, I saw your King sitting out on his porch at the top of the village, just as he does every day about that time. It was blisteringly hot. I hesitated to stop. In the end I parked my motor-bike on the verge and decided to risk it. My boldness has been amply rewarded. I made my way up through the village to let my old friend know that (for reasons of which you are aware) I was off to Ongola tomorrow. He generally gives me various commissions to execute on his behalf in town.

22

Then—you must believe this, Mama—a most extra-ordinary thing happened. Hardly had I sat down beside the King when, to my utter astonishment, he hesitantly stretched out one hand, as though afraid, towards the devotional objects I was carrying. There was an innocent quality of supplication about this gesture which I simply can't put into words—it was full of such modesty and humility. I would never have dreamed of finding either in the man. If only you could have seen your King at this moment—your beloved Bantu King! There he was, prac-tically begging me to make him a present of a scapular. Mama, I couldn't, under any circumstances, give him a consecrated scapular. Yet, if I had to revise the decision I fancy I might have acted differently. All I could do at the time was to make a formal promise of one on my return from Ongola. This promise both calmed and delighted him.

No doubt you will wonder what on earth I am worrying about. Believe me, Mama, there's more in this incident than meets the eye. I have a strange presentiment about it. To be honest, I haven't really got over it yet myself. The man I saw had nothing in common with the gross figure you have come to recognise from my letters—the palm-wine swiller, the oaf who picks up a whole leg of mutton in his bare hands and sits there gnawing away at it, talk-ing the whole time with his mouth crammed-full, telling filthy jokes to his admiring harem. This might have been a different man entirely.

I ask myself what can possibly have come over him? I think I know the answer. Is this presumptuous? It seems to me that our Saviour has at long last remembered my existence. Surely it isn't possible that He should remain deaf for ever to the prayers of his humble and faithful servants? How could I ever have faltered in my hope?

I had been waiting for so long that I had begun to despair. Everything has happened as I dreamed it would—and in the simplest, most unexpected way imaginable.

Truly God acts strangely. I don't know how to convey to you my joy, Mama. If only I could share it with you, here in Essazam, among these simple folk beginning at last to see the light of God, how utterly happy I should be!

Imagine it! Your Bantu King consenting to be baptised! Do you see what it means, Mama? It means Christ riding in all His glory through the loftiest gate of the New Jeru-salem. It means that, despite the thousands of years that have passed since His Ascension, Jesus is triumphant. I see the procession; the ecstatic, white-clad ranks of the faithful; I hear clear children's voices singing to celebrate the advent of the True God, the death of all vain supersti-tion. . . .

It was both a surprise and pleasure to learn that Father Drumont—as you describe him now, "an old man with-drawn from the world into pious meditation"—has visited you at home. (I can't stop myself adding the words "at home".) The Reverend Father Drumont: well, well! You know how much I have always admired this "old man". My regard has never weakened. I feel sure that age has done him all the good you say. Particularly brought to him that humility of which, I confess, he stood in need.

Perhaps I am a little hard on him? That is not because, from my long experience of mission-work, I judge our friend in a spirit of superiority. Do you remember the letters I wrote to you ten years ago, when he was passing through his spiritual crisis? You will recall I expressed doubts—not for long, it is true—about the sincerity of his faith. He was a proud and violent man. Prone to rebellion and despair. I felt that no Christian could be allowed such powers as his. Much less claim the destiny of the Church rested upon his shoulders. Do not forget, Mama, what Father Drumont did. Most improperly magnified his private and personal failure into a problem of shatter-ing dimensions.

My bitterest recollection is of his attempt (unconscious,

perhaps) to saddle the young among us with responsibility for the failure of a generation whose actions were based upon a mistaken, most un-Christian view. I owed nothing to the said generation. Shared none of its views. Neither do the increasing number of young people in Africa. They desire to bring their black cousins to Christianity from sincerest feelings of brotherhood.

Darling Mama, I can only hope that your well-ordered mind will forgive my rhetorical style, my unctuous sentiments. Believe me, I struggle against these faults every time I write. I know you will pin them down within two decimals!

Essazam, July 1948.

While Le Guen was writing this letter, something extraordinary was going on in the Palace. An atmosphere of panic and disaster built up like a tidal wave. It broke, ebbed a little, then surged back with renewed violence. The victims of its full impact were the more eminent elders of the clan. Following their usual evening custom, they assembled in the Chief's large drawing-room, waiting for him to join them. They talked, drank, and—with luck—ate until it was time to go home to bed. At the moment they were extremely nervous, attempting to conceal this by vying with one another in telling personal anecdotes. These stories were frequently interrupted by ponderous aphorisms. Each digression ended upon a careful hearty laugh. Its undertones carried chronic anxiety.

Most of the men looked very old and pitiable. They were seated upon benches drawn up to the bare walls; on the concrete floor in the centre of the room stood a hurricane-lamp. Its yellowish light cast their shadows upon the walls, turning some into giants and some into dwarfs. Its distortions invariably producing a grotesque effect. Every evening for years now they had gathered in the same room. It had never occurred to them that the sequence of events might one day be altered. The most distressing thing of all was their technique for combating panic.

Their most loquacious orator was certainly Ondoua. He regarded himself as the *doyen* of the clan—indeed, of the whole Essazam tribe. Age had robbed him of very little of his natural energy. It had augmented the flowery profusion of his language. As each speaker fell silent, Ondoua picked up from where he had left off. Perhaps he aimed at illuminating what had been said with the rare light of his genius. Perhaps his concern was to embellish every facet of discussion with precious detail forgotten by everyone bar himself. To listen, one would suppose he had seen everything, heard everything, visited every part of the country and was personally acquainted with each individual member of the tribe. He thought it inconceivable that he should be unaware of even the smallest or most recent event within tribal boundaries.

He never lost an opportunity of winning applause. His entire life centred round emulation. The previous elder statesman of the tribe had been Onana, from whom he had learnt much. When the old man died, Ondoua inherited his public functions. He not only appointed himself guide and mentor to the Ebazok clan, but attempted to extend his influence to the whole tribe. Here he came up against an equally ambitious old man, with the portentous name of Ndibidi. He claimed to be just as old and experienced as his rival, but belonged to a different clan. For several months competition had been intense. It was a question of which could talk louder, pronounce the greater number of prophecies. And, above all, establish claim to prediction—after an event had taken place.

Ondoua presided over the Palace *soirée* every evening. As usual, his was by far the most audible voice.

The tribal tax-collector Mekanda sat watching the old man with considerable distrust—more than was explained by Ondoua's lack of enthusiasm for paying his family taxes. (These referred mainly to his two sons, notorious cowards, regarded by most people as mere grown-up louts.) Mekanda's short spell at school had produced in him instinctive suspicion of patriarchs as a class, and of Ondoua in particular.

Also among those present was Ezoum the Catechist, Le Guen's representative in the inner council of the clan. He was a very tall and extremely ugly person, who hid himself in the darkest corner of the room. Besides being a sanctimonious prig and village Tartuffe, he had an uncommon gift for anticipating people's conversation. He would listen and bide his time; then, like the Good Samaritan he took himself to be, choose the exact moment for support. He would point out that what was being proposed had parallel and authority in Holy Writ.

The night was well advanced, but the elders maintained their drawing-room vigil. Finally a door creaked open and the whole company fell silent. A white-hot globe of fire moved slowly forward, breaking up the shadows, stripping the walls back to their chalk-pale lustre, hissing as it moved, blinding to the eye. The pressure-lamp advanced into the middle of the room, trailing behind it a strange shadow. This seemed a parody of a human figure until it resolved itself into an immensely tall, flat-chested woman, as long and dry as an old spear-shaft.

The men screwed up their eyes, staring at the brilliant light and the shadow that seemed to be attached to it. The woman's face was narrow, lacking depth, with high, prominent cheek-bones behind wrinkled cheeks. There was more anger than distress in her expression. She was not so much sad, as fierce. Having set the lamp on the ground, she moved a little to one side and eyed the gathering, as though seeking a victim to devour. There she stood in the middle of the room, a virago wearing a badly cut flowered dress, mercilessly revealing her shrunken thighs, scrawny buttocks and other unfortunate points. She spluttered and coughed, either in an attempt to clear her throat or as a face-saving device. She had never before been called upon to announce a piece of bad news.

"He—he won't be coming!" she exclaimed finally, in a quavering voice. It sounded as though she were holding her breath, trying to imitate a very sick person, whose every word cost vast effort.

Though Ondoua had more presence of mind than the rest, he was shaken. "*What* did you say, Makri?" he gasped.

It had been sufficient to see Makrita in the house at all at this late hour, let alone by the Chief's bedside. How well their fears were justified. Clearly Essomba was not himself. Perhaps some sort of disaster was imminent?

"I tell you he won't be coming tonight," the woman repeated, more distinctly. Her chilly authority seemed greater.

Her every inflexion, even her cough, carried reproof. This was the Chief's first wife, the one he had married as a young man. It goes without saying he had not chosen her himself. For years now she had been watching and waiting, praying to heaven for a day of victory such as this. Though she did not appear so on the surface, she was triumphant. In vain had she shed tears before every wise elder of the clan and, when that failed, of the tribe. She had recounted the misery and injustice of her lot. Her attitude to these old dotards had transformed into angry contempt. She upbraided them for their futility. "I may have been kicked out of the bridal bed to make way for younger women," she would remark, "but when there's a real crisis I shall be the one who answers the call."

And so when the Chief (still hardly aware of being ill) found crisis upon him, he dragged himself to Makri's house rather than that of one of his other wives. Makri lit a big fire and settled him in her humble bed. He showed confidence in the loving solicitude of this rejected woman, who took it hard being his wife in no more than name.

Makri said, with finality: "He won't be coming. You'd all better go home. The Chief won't be here because he's ill—very seriously ill."

"Ill? The Chief? Ill?" An incredulous muttering rippled round the room. One or two present declared their intention of going to the sick man's bedside and questioning him. What were his initial symptoms? Had it come upon him suddenly, or had he suffered a long time without telling anyone? This suggestion was not only rash in the extreme, but one their ancestors would have condemned.

Ondoua had an infallible cure up his sleeve. Just the thing to remove this minor indisposition overnight. All he needed was for someone, preferably the Chief himself, to give an exact description of the symptoms. Ezoum the Catechist wanted to spend the night kneeling by the sick man's bed reciting the Rosary. "In a low voice, of course," he hastily added. Makrita dealt firmly with such senile suggestions. She convinced them that their schemes would be valueless. She radiated energy and resourcefulness, making it clear she intended to look after the Chief herself. It was surprising how quickly they relinquished pet ideas. Perhaps they were secretly relieved?

The Reverend Father Le Guen, Superior of the Catholic Mission at Essazam, retired leaving his desk littered with numerous lengthy letters written that evening. Before his departing for Ongola the following morning he set about folding up these letters, putting them into envelopes and stamping them.

He had just reached the stamp-licking stage when a boy slipped into the room. A tall, skinny child, more thoughtful in appearance than the usual run of Mission boys. His innocent words contrasted piquantly with his serious expression.

"One pair of shoes will for you enough be, Father?" he enquired, "or another must I polish?"

"My God," murmured Le Guen, without turning round to look at the boy, "what a paragon of elocution you are! Repeat what you have just said, please."

The child hesitated, not sure if he was to obey literally, or whether this was just another of Le Guen's regular jokes.

"Come on, boy," the latter coaxed. "Repeat what you said just then. Repeat it *exactly*. Show me you haven't been wasting time over your grammar. Preserve all your intriguing inversions: it's not fair, if you don't. Now then!"

The boy decided to humour Le Guen: this was a joke. Spacing out not only the words but the syllables he said: "One pair of shoes will for you enough be, Father, or another must I polish?"

At last Le Guen turned. "What a scholar you are, Gustave! Ten out of ten."

His expression registered the happy complacency of a paterfamilias bursting with pride at his son's precocity. His eyes were moist with gratified tenderness. His laugh ended as a hearty guffaw, shaking his full beard in gusts of mirth. On few occasions had Le Guen felt morally self-satisfied; most often, when observing this boy's gradual progress. When he had taken him into the Mission House a few years back, the child had been a nonentity. Le Guen taught him French, with some success. The boy now spoke with Le Guen's accent and inflexions. He was even developing his teacher's private mannerisms.

"How old are you now?" Le Guen asked.

"Twelve, Father. Why?"

The boy was a kind of sensitised plate, faithfully reproducing every influence. The linguistic affectations of Joseph Schloegel, for instance. That increasingly insistent "Why?" which the boy tagged at the end of his answers to questions. Le Guen recognised the turn of phrase peculiar to the regrettable Brother Joseph.

He began to consider Brother Joseph. Generally he abstained from this, having a well-developed sense of charity He fought a worried suspicion of the boy. How far had this imitation of Schloegel developed? Was it well advanced or still in the early stages? Schloegel's free-and-easy manners and equally free-and-easy morals caused a certain amount of notoriety.

Le Guen wanted to get this painful business over as soon as possible. He came close, bent over the boy, held his hand. No longer laughing, Le Guen blushed a little as he prepared to go through that shameful subterfuge whereby parents pretend to place children on a common footing, when, in fact, they are making fools of them. He hesitated, uncertain of his line. He was about to trot out a very well-worn excuse to the boy. Gustave might see through this. How to convince the child that he *could not* take him on the journey? That Ongola was no place for children?

Already the Bishop had a large personal staff and strongly objected to guests accompanied by their own house-boys. Every possible service and convenience was assured. But the Episcopal Palace had no accommodation available for house-boys.

Each time that Le Guen was leaving for Ongola, the boy felt an uncontrollable wanderlust. This emotion was never, alas, satisfied. Le Guen lacked sufficient courage to brave the Bishop's irritation. Poor Gustave always spent a long, unhappy week on his own.

"Why?" Le Guen repeated, picking the conversation up at the point where they had left it. The boy stared at him, wide-eyed and innocent, trying to pretend he was still a little piccaninny. "Why? Well, you speak French so well now I hardly know you. Understand?"

Quite honestly the boy did not. He shook his head to

signify as much. Le Guen sat down, pulling him on to his knee.

"Listen, Gustave. Try to put yourself in my place. Remember the tiny scrap you were when you first came to live here. Do you remember?"

"Do I remember?" the boy exclaimed, perking up. "I remember all right; clear as clear. I can just see myself. It's true, I *was* a tiny little thing, even tinier than I am now——"

"Yes, yes. Anything else?"

"I used to cry with fright in my room at bedtime and I wanted to go home to the village and my mother. When I served at table I broke all the plates, so you got the cook back to wait on you instead. Since then I haven't had anything to do. Well, nothing much, at least."

"Nothing to do, eh? That isn't what your friend the cook tells me, you know. He says he's very pleased with your behaviour. You help him a lot, I hear. It seems you're plucky and willing to run errands. He even informs me that you're responsible for making the beds now."

"Yes, that's right," the boy said and added, mischievously: "I know how to ring bells now, too."

At this point Le Guen burst out laughing, despite himself. The boy, assuming an expression of intense embarrassment, joined in cheerfully enough.

"Do you still remember that morning?" Le Guen asked him.

"I'll say I do! Couldn't forget it."

"You know what you looked like? A little chick being carried off by a sparrow-hawk. Or in your case, a bell-rope. You held your own very well, for a chick. You hung on to that rope like grim death—straining and tugging as hard as you could. The bell swung you clean off your feet every time, but it made no difference to you, did it?"

The boy exhaled. He said, "I remember, I've come a long way since then. I don't break dishes any more while

32

I'm washing up. I don't wet my bed. I'm not scared in the dark before I go to sleep. I don't even bother you to take me to Ongola any more," he wound up triumphantly.

Before Le Guen recovered from his astonishment, the boy changed the subject. "I went down to the village after Mass this morning. My mother had another baby last night."

"I don't believe it!"

"It's true, all right. That's where I've just been."

"Well, which was it?"

The child pulled a face. "Oh, only a girl. But that isn't all. The Chief's ill."

"Ill? No danger with that one, my child. When he's poured a gallon or so of palm-wine down his gullet you'll see him get up as fresh as a daisy."

The boy shook his head firmly several times in dissent.

"It isn't the same thing this time, Father," he said, seriously. "The Chief has taken to his bed. Since last night."

Le Guen stared, his attention caught more by the child's small face, on which an expression of gravity sat most becomingly, than by what he had said. Le Guen did not take Gustave's announcement seriously.

"You shouldn't go away—not now," the boy insisted.

"Why do you say such things, laddie? You know very well the Chief is *never* ill, don't you? Well, then!"

"Father, it's always the same with people who've never had a day's illness all their life. The first time they fall sick, that's it. They never get up again. *I* think the Chief's done for, by the look of it."

Then the boy hesitated. Le Guen knew, without admitting it, that Gustave was reporting what the natives said down in the village. He could imitate *their* style, too, when he had a mind to do so.

"You don't abandon a dying friend," Gustave said, in a

33

calm, peremptory voice. "The Chief was your close friend, wasn't he?"

For the first time Le Guen seemed genuinely disconcerted. He began to tug at his beard and wipe his lips with the back of his hand. Just then an engine suddenly burst into life outside. First the cylinders fired slowly, then faster, until with much back-firing, the motor sighed to a standstill again. Peace fell upon the morning sunshine.

Le Guen leant briefly out of the window to watch Brother Joseph's difficulties, and came to the boy, placing both hands upon his shoulders.

"Listen, child: the Bishop expects me tomorrow, do you understand? Tomorrow at eleven o'clock precisely. With any luck that decrepit old Tin Lizzie should get us to Ongola tonight. I ought to reach the Palace tomorrow morning, just in time to answer my name, when it's called. And it's essential, absolutely essential, that I *am* there on time. Does that kind of necessity mean anything to you?"

The words were addressed not to Gustave alone but, through him, to everyone in the village. The boy would certainly plead Le Guen's cause with the locals.

Two brisk knocks sounded.

"Come in, Brother Joseph," Le Guen called. Schloegel had only bothered to knock for form's sake. Already he had turned the doorknob and was in the room before being invited. He removed his topee, more to mop his forehead than from politeness. He was a brusque man. Manners were not his strongest point.

"The engine's not going too well, Your Reverence," he announced, blowing out his breath in defeat,

"I know. I heard Lizzie doing her best. Did you have the throttle wide open?"

"Yes. No good at all."

"Well, that's that, then."

34

"Too true," Schloegel agreed. "Let's leave the old bus to Raphael; he's just dying to get his hands on her."

"Raphael? Raphael who?"

"You know—the joker who was at Kufra——"

"Ah yes, I remember. You think we can rely on him?"

"Certainly. He's terrific. The Hero of Kufra, you know. Joking apart, he does seem to know about the innards of cars. If he can put life into this crocked-up old motor it'll be quite something. Heavens, what a ramshackle engine it has! I'm relying on Raphael. The internal combustion engine appears to be his main interest in life."

The two men turned to Gustave. The child was squatting in one corner of the room, calmly and industriously polishing a pair of brown shoes. With self-restraint he refrained from speech, but he took care to stay within range of their conversation.

"This creature," said Le Guen to Schloegel, "has just been telling me—can you imagine it?—that we shouldn't go."

"He also? Well, well! Raphael was harping on the same theme a few moments ago. He reproached me for abandoning my old friend at death's door——"

"The old friend, I take it, being the Chief?"

"If we're to believe Raphael," Brother Joseph said, "the Chief's in a really bad way. He's been bedridden since yesterday evening. Something, it seems, which has never happened. Raphael took great care to emphasise that. He seems to think anyone who's ill enough to go to bed is automatically done for. By the way, how old *is* the Chief, do you suppose?"

"It's hard to guess. When you ask people their age in these parts, the old add a few years for the fun of it. In contrast the young knock quite a bit off. *He* says he's seen nearly six score seasons, as he puts it. Then you have to add those he can't remember because he was too young.

35

That gives you a round figure of, let's say, a hundred and thirty seasons."

"Yes, but what does he mean by a 'season'?"

"A season, here, is the period between sowing and harvest. Two seasons every year, since they sow and reap twice within twelve months."

"A fortunate country, eh?"

"Just so! By this reckoning the Chief would be sixty-five, which is obviously an exaggeration. You've only to look at him."

"Why is it an exaggeration?" Schloegel asked.

"Well, think! He's got twenty-three wives. Has fun and games with the whole lot of them every night. He's never left off sowing his wild oats. *Sixty-five?* Don't make me laugh! If that was true, he'd have been dead by now."

"I humbly apologise, Your Reverence. I don't dispute that he's got twenty-three wives. What he does with them is quite another matter."

"That's unimportant; a minor detail. All I know is, you've only to look at the man to see he isn't sixty-five. Sixty-five years leave their mark on a man——"

"And on a woman, too. They must last better here than at home. Well, why not? They don't give a damn about anything. Wives are left to do all the work—especially the Chief's. No worries, no emotional strain; a nicely balanced nervous system. No need to come to daily grips with complicated industrial problems. Gives them quite an advantage, Your Reverence."

The car's engine roared into life again. For a moment it stuttered uncertainly. Then its sound became strong and clear. The two missionaries looked at one another, astonished.

"It looks as though we're all right to go," Schloegel ventured.

"That is exactly my opinion. In fact," Le Guen added, with ponderous wit, "I *part*ake of it." Schloegel often

36

made puns and jokes of this sort. Le Guen wanted to show he also could rise to the occasion.

They hurried downstairs, the boy at their heels, and found Raphael sitting at the wheel of the ancient van, fiddling with the controls, his whole body vibrating to the rhythm of the engine. The Hero of Kufra looked more cheerfully hilarious than ever. Surprisingly he woke every morning happier than when he went to bed.

When he saw them, he slammed a lightning uppercut at the gear-lever and, with equal briskness, jumped his foot off the clutch. The van emitted a tortured howl, terminating in a crack like a pistol-shot enough to scare twenty bemedalled colonels. For a moment the wheels spun wildly, then the van shot forward and bounced clean off the ground to descend again, tyres first, with a metallic crash. It sounded as though the whole thing was coming to pieces.

Raphael obviously thought himself back upon some sandy caravan track in the Libyan desert. Roaring with laughter, his huge white teeth revealed in a melon-splitting grin, he turned the wheel this way and that, accelerating the whole time. Despite his efforts to control this infernal machine, he seemed a mere passenger. Yet there was a certain sense about the way he twisted and turned and shot round corners. Will-power, perhaps, confined him to the boundaries of the square before the Mission House.

The onlookers who had collected hastily took cover. Some retreated into the church. The men shouted, the women uttered faint screams of alarm. Le Guen grinned cheerfully. Above the din Schloegel roared, "The drunken sot! He's going to pile her up! *Raphael, for God's sake, you stupid bastard!*" The Hero of Kufra was unconcerned. After all, he had made Lizzie go in the first place. He was quite justified in claiming a generous reward.

It could not go on for ever. Lizzie apparently decided

to do no more. Independently of Raphael, she turned her nose in the opposite direction. After a brief hesitation, she went straight for the missionaries, who retreated at speed. Just when they both had visions of lying lifeless in the dust beneath her wheels, Lizzie stopped. The radiator-cap flew off with a sonorous clang and rattled away. Raphael greeted this development with a burst of laughter equally sonorous but louder.

Eye-witnesses found difficulty in retaining composure. The missionaries climbed into the van. Judging by his language, Schloegel was the more shaken. Never again, he swore, would he allow anyone to talk him into trusting his beloved Lizzie to the Hero of Kufra or anyone like him.

Gustave leant in at Le Guen's door and asked, as a special favour, to be allowed to ride his bicycle.

"Angelic child!" Le Guen exclaimed playfully. "Of *course* you can." Ready to face any unforeseen situation, including martyrdom, he managed to preserve equanimity.

He gave the impression of being in a mood to say "Yes" indiscriminately. When the choir ladies approached him with a petition not to return without the big harmonium he had promised so long ago, Le Guen waved in such a way as to suggest friendly agreement. The effect was rather spoilt as the van chose this moment to start. Le Guen's gesture was confined to a sketchy flapping with the left hand. A cloud of dust enveloped them as the van dwindled into the distance.

The Hero of Kufra had been responsible for yet another shambles.

Within a few days the Chief passed all the milestones which, according to Essazam belief, marked the road to the eternal bonfire. After displaying symptoms of fever he had taken at once to his bed. This indicated that the illness was critical. In this tribe no one was deemed sick as long as he could stand up unsupported and walk on his own two legs. That he might have a limb nearly rotted off with gangrene was irrelevant.

Soon after Le Guen and Schloegel had set off for Ongola, the Chief ceased to take nourishment. This he had done from time to time, out of caprice. He also forswore his beloved palm-wine. Previously this had acted as an infallible medicine whenever he felt indisposed. Moreover it was his most pleasurable self-indulgence. No one could imagine his doing without it or recall a previous abstention—even under stress of bereavement.

Everyone accordingly assumed him doomed shortly to cross the River and rejoin his ancestors. This rumour of imminent catastrophe spread like wildfire to the most distant village of the Essazam tribe. The elders of every clan, wishing to be present during the last moments of their blood-brother and great Chief, left home, starting off on the long trek through the forest.

Next day the Chief became delirious. Shortly afterwards he displayed other symptoms; indifference to his surroundings and visitors. Also permanent refusal or inability to speak, often harbinger of a dying man's last breath. He was prostrate and helpless. His condition bore out the popular belief that people who were never ill tended to snuff out like candles when the time came.

Panic descended upon Essazam. Drummers squatted over their tom-toms, mournful, assiduous, sending endless messages through the dense jungle, begging all witch-doctors and medicine-men, whatever their tribe or creed, to rally and save the Chief in his dire need. Day and night the forest glades trembled and re-echoed to the thunderous rhythm of drums. Messages seemed relayed, not from village to village, but from one bush to another.

This drama was played against the background of an interminable violent storm. Thunder and lightning, accompanied by torrential rain, ripped through the jungle. Trees were struck, crops devastated, houses stripped of roofs. Women and children were caught up in violent gusts of wind, whirled along, then tossed aside and abandoned. Nature seemed to have decided to isolate the Chief still further upon the desolate island of sickness. This man, who had spent his life surrounded by courtiers, was now being cut adrift from Life's mainland and relinquished, body and soul, into the hands of Death.

Hardly had the storm died away than the first emissaries from the clans reached Essazam—people who had heard the news first, walked fastest, or came from the nearest villages.

A dismal atmosphere greeted them. There were men, who had not eaten for several days, sitting about in listless dejection; women who had given up all pretence of looking after their homes or fields; women silent save for telling willing listeners how friends, children or they themselves had been transported by invisible beings to the depths of the forest, then, by lucky accident, rescued. There were wretched children, too scared to play after hearing tales of horror recounted by their little friends. The latter claimed to have seen the Chief's ghost in the heart of the whirlwind, shrieking and grimacing, hands bound behind his back, his head hanging upon his chest. They affirmed that he was whimpering, screaming, and writhing as if under repeated blows of the lash. They had heard the whistle and crack of whips curling round his body. They had not, however, been able to identify the faces of his torturers.

The wise men treated such hallucinations seriously. They believed them to be accurate premonitions. Thus they had an unfortunate influence upon the whole town. It was gripped by inertia. The new arrivals were no more immune than the rest.

Particularly noticeable among them was one old woman. Incredibly ancient, with a long scrawny neck in which the veins and arteries stood out like rope, she had skin not so much wrinkled as *threadbare*. All her life she had struggled with the soil, turning it, breaking it, bent over it with a hoe. The soil had rubbed the nap off her in turn. Thick roots and tree-stumps also had lent a hand, as she had cleared a meagre space among them to plant maize, cassava and sugar-cane. Thickets and thorn-bushes had scored and scratched her as she toiled through the jungle providing her livelihood. She had clearly suffered also from the attentions of men, who had used her till she was an ugly, worn-out crone.

Her thin, shrivelled lips revealed a fine set of long, narrow teeth. (This was unusual: most of the Essazam had thick, stumpy teeth, close-packed.) Yellow-stained from chewing tobacco, they chattered continuously— the result of a senile tic in the lower jaw. Nevertheless, the old woman's eyes were sharp and hawk-like. She was bundled up in a kind of voluminous robe. This enfolded her skeletal body like a sack, secured at the waist by a thick cord, below which it hung to her knees in countless bunched pleats. Beneath this garment emerged scrawny legs, with two incredible feet resembling artists' palettes, only slightly longer than they were wide. Her pointed toes, curving inwards like those of a chimpanzee, were equipped with long, sharp nails reminiscent of a vulture's claws. To these permanent marks of misery she added ones appropriate to her forthcoming bereavement. Her head was close-shaven and covered with ashes; these she had also rubbed over her face, feet, and the lower part of her legs. About her neck hung a large rosary.

A frail skiff tossed upon seas of grief, she fluttered from end to end of the village in a trance-like state, unburdening her soul by general confession. Out came a flood of verbosity. Every intimate secret of her past life was revealed, all her repressed instincts and passions. As she drifted across the square, chattering away, calling

41

upon God and her ancestors, cursing, threatening, blaspheming, openly accusing those she held guilty of this tragedy, her view of events assumed a more precise shape. Yosifa—this was the old woman's name—refused to believe the illness. It was inconceivable, she declared, in a man who had enjoyed continual good health. She compared the Chief's constitution to a pool in a woodland glade, its surface unruffled by a single dead leaf. Sometimes, she continued, a child—through playfulness or malice—threw some object into the water just to see the ripples circle and break up that crystalline surface. This was what she believed had happened in the present case. Not a child this time, but an adult, well aware what he was about, had performed a similar action. This had destroyed the unbroken good health of her beloved nephew, the Chief of the Essazam.

Ever since the early days of his illness the Essazam elders, reinforced by those from other villages of the Ebazok clan to which the Chief himself belonged, had gathered at the Palace soon after dawn. Here they sat, side by side, on long wooden benches on the verandah around the building. They gossiped about this and that while they waited—nobody was quite sure for what. Shoulder to shoulder they sat, heads lolling, eyes turned vacantly towards the setting sun. They chewed betel and passed round a snuff-box or a rank-smelling calabash pipe. Occasionally one of their wives, in a frenzy of solicitude, brought something to eat—a leg of chicken several days old, a hastily prepared bowl of groundnut porridge, or cob of roasted maize. The food was at once shared.

When the first delegates from other clans appeared, these resident elders made room for them by squeezing closer together on the benches. Their womenfolk, who had turned out in equal numbers, were directed to Makrita's house, where the Chief lay dying. They joined

42

the local ladies. These had grown tired of nursing a man obviously doomed to die anyway and were beginning to weep for him instead—a mild prelude to the orgy of groans and despairing howls they would loose when he breathed his last. Between one burst of lamentation and the next, they bestowed a few words of comfort upon his unfortunate wives.

The ancient frenzied crone, Yosifa, burst upon the circle of elders round the Palace, a raving visitor from the outside heat of the day. She burned and glowed like a sunstruck serpent. She turned violently upon each of them, shrieking in that harshly raucous voice characteristic of feminine hysteria: "Confess! Confess that you murdered him, you false friend, you traitor, you nothingness! My God, it's true, you *have* murdered him! Admit it! Look at him, all of you. Look at the creature, the assassin who did away with my beloved child! What was it drove you? Jealousy? Or desire? You itched to have his lovely wives for yourself, didn't you? And those huge plantations of his, eh? And that magnificent Palace. His big strongboxes, crammed with gold—you desired them all, didn't you? That's why you killed him, isn't it? Tell us how you went about the job—was it poison you used, or did you have a little bedroom intrigue?"

Subjected to this outburst, some of the elders pretended that they neither saw nor heard Yosifa. Others shrank away from sight rather than face the offensive, vitriolic drivel being poured out. However, one observed with indulgent forbearance: "Yosifa—dear sister—how can you talk in this way? You don't know what you're saying; sorrow has blinded you. How can you accuse *us*? We have always loved our brother and Chief more dearly than our own lives. We would do anything in our power to heal his sickness. Really, you don't know what you're saying. Yosi, dear sister, please, please calm yourself——"

Far from placated, the old woman, hawk-eyes glinting,

cursed them in a louder voice than before, panting and raving with increased fury. Finally Ezoum, the local Catechist, approached her. Despite his prim austerity, he had a persuasive, honey-sweet tongue.

Taking Yosifa by the hand he said: "Yosifa: in the name of Jesus, who came down among us to deliver us from our sins, in the name of the Blessed Virgin who suffered the supreme martyrdom of seeing her Son die on the Cross, I beseech you, remember that Christian precept bidding us ensure that our accusations are well-founded before bearing witness against our neighbour. Dear sister, cease these idle accusations! You have no proof of what you say. Go instead to your son's bedside."

"Where is he, then?" the old crone panted. "Is he dead already? Take me to where he lies. Your words are just: you speak with the voice of God Himself. I was wrong to accuse these men. I didn't know what I was saying. But—but *someone* must have done it, even so——"

With the exception of Makrita, who kept a constant bedside vigil, the Chief's wives at first devoted themselves energetically to succouring their lord and master. They had combed the bush and the jungle for such herbs and plants as the medicine-men demanded. They had scurried the whole length and breadth of the countryside in their zeal to obtain anything conceivably of help. As the disease progressed unchecked, without openly admitting it, they concluded that the Chief was under sentence of death and relinquished their efforts. They formed the habit of squatting upon Makri's verandah. A pathetic sight they made, poor droopy creatures huddled upon the concrete floor, backs to the wall, knees drawn up to their chins, faces buried in their laps. They never noticed the old woman's arrival upon the arm of Ezoum the Catechist. It may be said in passing that he had made advances to all of them in his time and had without exception been turned down.

Yosifa sighted them as she was going up the stairs to the

sickroom. She commenced a fresh performance of her act, accusing them of murdering her son and various other crimes.

"Admit it, you witch, you sorceress!" the old harridan shrieked. "Admit you assassinated him! Vile intriguer, accursed strumpet! What poisonous juices have you squeezed into your cooking today? Everyone knows your clan is a solid nest of murderers—you had ample opportunity to learn your craft. Come on, tell me, which evil spirits are you invoking at the moment?"

This time Ezoum the Catechist, man of God, chose not to intervene. The old woman discharged her venom against the Chief's wretched wives at leisure, without interruption. The victims broke into silent sobs. Tears poured down their cheeks, following furrows worn by tears already shed.

Then Yosifa turned on an inoffensive young girl, small, scared, plump, hardly more than a child and pregnant into the bargain. This was the latest arrival, the Chief's twenty-third wife. She could not stand the old woman's invective for long. Suddenly she ran round the corner of the house, like a hunted hare, to hide in the plantation and have a good cry.

Yosifa only calmed down when inside the house and confronted by its occupant. His eyes were wide open. He retained some degree of consciousness, but had long since passed into another world, remote, serene, and lay there, dumb, apathetic, his wasted face expressionless.

Did he recognise old Yosi, his mother? After looking at her two or three times from the corner of one eye, he firmly turned aside his head.

Makri sat beside him. Her attitude, no longer that of a vigilant nurse, was rather of one watching over the dead. For several moments Yosi stood speechless, confronted by what seemed her son's corpse. Her lips trembled, the tic becoming exaggerated.

45

Suddenly she launched into an interminable series of frantic gestures, genuflecting, crossing herself, beating her breast, prostrating herself upon the ground. The procedure was punctuated with sighs, groans, tearful prayers and similar signs of mental unbalance. Makrita and the Catechist watched, alarmed.

As they observed her, Yosifa abruptly raised one hand —bonier, more tremulous than ever—to her throat. With a stiff, jerky gesture she removed the rosary. With some difficulty, since the Chief was almost as stiff as a corpse, she placed his hands together, winding the rosary about them in a deathbed fetish.

At this point occurred the most surprising incident of the Chief's serious illness, one which was to have unforeseeable consequences, not only for the whole tribe, but for specific individuals, such as the absent Le Guen.

It was a little thing, really. Her demented spasm approached its climax. Yosifa said: "He has been baptised, hasn't he?"

Makrita shook her head. The Catechist took the old woman by the arm, trying unsuccessfully to make her drop the point. The Chief had firmly resisted all such attempts. While still able to make decisions he argued against baptism. This merely set her off howling worse than ever.

"What?" she screamed, "what? You villains, you murderers, you mean to tell me you haven't baptised him? It's a plot. You've let him die as though he was just anybody! Ezoum, my friend, I'll have you broken for this when Le Guen gets back. He'll wipe the floor with you. Call yourself a *Catechist*!"

Yosifa screamed, sobbed and fairly danced with rage. Nothing quietened her. She even bared her teeth, as though about to bite someone, and rolled upon the ground. Hearing this din, a number of people, thinking the Chief actually dead, rushed round. Some managed to enter the

46

house. The rest, unable to squeeze through, hung about outside. There was considerable noise, elbowing and confused hubbub. Crude energy was exerted, unsuccessfully to make Yosifa understand the situation.

Grimly determined, gestures stiffer and more jerky than ever, the old woman came close to the sick man. He gave her one glance, promptly losing interest again. He neither moved nor shook his head. Perhaps he was too weak.

Flabbergasted silence fell upon the crowd as Yosifa said to the Chief: "Son, are you willing for me to baptise you? You are, aren't you? Tell me that you accept this baptism, my son." The invalid remained motionless, more out of reach than ever. His expression retained a faint flicker of life. Without ado Yosifa picked up a cup from the foot of the big wooden bed. Hastily filling it with water, she brandished it in mid-air and emptied it over the Chief's head. This ritual she repeated several times, trembling and mumbling over the accompanying words, as though to convince herself that he was being truly baptised. "I baptise you in the name of the Father . . ."

The Chief lay stiff and remote as ever, his wide-open eyes staring vacantly at the ceiling. Yosifa feverishly filled and emptied cup after cup upon him. She might have continued until dropping from sheer exhaustion if a certain male onlooker had not shown presence of mind by forcibly removing her. As she was carried out those present heard her muttering, over and over again, "At least I've got him baptised."

The boy Gustave had witnessed the entire scene. He spent hours puzzling out its meaning.

The influx of visitors had almost doubled the population of Essazam. When night fell the older men traditionally set about billeting new arrivals, as guests, upon various village families. Old Yosifa was entertained by the Chief's youngest wife. Anaba took her to her little house across from the Palace and did her generous best to make the old harridan comfortable. Peaceful and satisfied, Yosifa seemed to have forgotten the charges recently levelled against Anaba. In fact she treated the girl to a cosily intimate monologue.

"Well, child," she said, "so you're my boy's new wife, eh? What a lovely creature you are, to be sure! Turn this way, let me have a good look at you. That's better. You're the prettiest of the lot, my girl. Of course, I haven't seen you before. Wasn't at the wedding, was I? Listen to me, child. I've been at death's door for years now, yet every day my old carcase increasingly resists attempts to shift it. It isn't the Chief who ought to die, but myself. No son should die before his mother. Still, since God wishes it so, let it be according to His will.

"You're so lovely, I can't take my eyes off you. He knew how to pick his women. He was above the common rut in everything. Lord, Lord, how this rheumatism pinches me. . . ."

Her mind wandered, then she said: "Look, forget the things I said to you. I didn't really mean them. What earthly reason would *you* have for killing him? You've hardly been in his household any time at all. Ah, child, if you'd been at my dear sister's deathbed, you'd understand my grief today. She entrusted her children to me, begged me to watch over them and raise them. I remember every word she said, just as though it were yesterday. She only had the two boys, but they were real *men*. I had eight hulking great kids. You'll see them all soon enough: they're due at any moment.

"Five grown-up boys, who don't give a damn for me. Can you believe it? The things we suffer in this life! What have I left, now that he's as good as dead? Oh, you can't imagine how loving and respectful he used to be to me, child. I often used to visit him in the days when I could still travel. As soon as he saw me at the end of the village,

48

he'd bounce up out of his chair, leave whatever he was doing. Even abandon his guests, however distinguished. He'd run across the square just to put his arms round my neck. Afterwards he entrusted Makrita with the task of looking after me. Oh, he was very concerned for my welfare. 'Take great care of my mother,' he told her. 'Cherish her always. Don't stint the chickens and goats where she's concerned.' And you know, Makri always followed his instructions to the letter. She could hardly have treated me disrespectfully, seeing that her husband honoured me as if I was his own mother. Oh no, she never fed *me* with the dog's scraps. . . . But maybe you'll be glad to take her place," the old woman concluded artlessly, "who knows?"

The following day a fresh batch of bigwigs from the Essazam clans arrived. Among them was a man who, despite advancing years, presented a solid, robust appearance. His bare torso was preceded by a monumental belly, its skin stretched drum-tight and gleaming like oiled silk. A ceremonial loin-cloth was secured round the plateau of his buttocks by a huge knot. His naked belly bounced up and down as he walked. He wore a kind of bright scarlet Phrygian cap, adorned with an outsize pompom. This pompom sat snugly between his coppery shoulders, attached to the centre of his headgear by a long cord. Its green was outrageously bright, splashing over the midday sunlight with the effect of a squirt of lemon juice. More from custom than need of support he leaned upon a spear with a long, flexible shaft tipped with a small steel point. Much handling had given the wood a curious patina; an elusive sheen that belonged to its owner's character. He flourished this strange weapon with rough-and-ready elegance of a vaguely ritual nature. The spear symbolised his official function as did the trident of Neptune.

The assembly gaped awesomely. When he deigned to uncover his head it was completely bald. Like most of the Essazam, he had enormous feet, wider than they were long. An additional peculiarity was that the horny skin round his toes was scored with innumerable deep cracks and lines. He was known as 'Ndibidi'—a well-deserved Bantu nickname meaning "Glutton".

On this occasion Ndibidi gave a full-scale display of "ham" acting. Directly he arrived he stumped warily around the Palace two or three times in quick succession, eyes fiery, nostrils dilated with ill-suppressed rage. He ignored the grouped elders, conveying an impression of stupefaction at the disaster befallen the tribe, and exaggerated caution in approaching representatives of this clan. His bearing challenged the Chief's entourage.

"They're guilty till they can prove themselves innocent," he seemed to be saying. "However it turns out, we'll have a long, profitable argument first. Meanwhile, one must be careful."

He looked as though there were no censure equal to the enormity of their crime.

Ndibidi was Chief Elder of the Edzogmekong clan. Its members referred to themselves as "The Friends of Peace". To the others they were known as "The Yellowbellies".

When he had made quite certain all eyes and ears were upon him, Ndibidi spoke, pacing up and down as he did so. "O men of the Ebazok clan!" he declaimed, "will you now, at long last, make up your minds to tell us what is going on here?" He mouthed the words with exaggerated pauses between them, waving his spear, flouncing his loincloth like a skirt, jerking his head and arm about. "You were his close companions, O men of the Ebazok clan. Will you have the kindness to tell us how things have come to this pass?"

He repeated the cloudy, improbable accusations old Yosifa had hurled at them the previous evening. He went about it with greater skill and fluency, using specialised idioms giving words different meaning and significance. He never lost an opportunity of referring to past tribal heroes.

This was not surprising, since glowing accounts of their deeds served him in lieu of rational argument. His persuasive powers, or the Essazam's love of mystery (even at their own expense), caused people to jump up at every stage of his rambling speech to endorse the vituperation he hurled at wretched Ebazok clansmen.

Ondoua, perceiving his rival's success, beckoned his ancient wife and whispered in her ear, his eye twinkling with malice. He merely told her to serve this fellow with all that remained of last night's roast porcupine. Ndibidi's gluttony led him straight into the trap. Directly he sat down and started to eat, Ondoua, who was awaiting the opportunity, rose ponderously, grabbed his rival's spear and promenaded round the house in exact imitation. He launched into a flow of equally colourful rhetoric, not so much to clear the Ebazok clansmen of Ndibidi's charges as to efface his rival's triumph. Essazam was his pigeon. He had to preserve his moral authority.

Much to everyone's surprise, for the rest of the day the Chief's condition remained much the same. That evening his daughter Cecilia arrived, slipping in furtively under cover of nightfall.

"Well, well," said Ndibidi. "That looked like Cecilia to me—the Chief's daughter by old Makri."

"Certainly it was," Ondoua agreed, tranquilly.

The two were sitting side by side on the Palace verandah.

"She's just back from the city. Someone must have passed on the news. Apparently she's a job there—making a packet of money, too. No one knows just what sort of a job. Reminds me of her brother, come to think of it."

"Youth today," Ndibidi announced, with great conviction, "is a mystery." He was not well equipped to understand the respective mentalities of a whore and a pimp.

The Chief's elder son, Maurice, was not only Cecilia's brother but also her "protector". He arrived late that night, drunk as usual. He announced his presence with loud denunciations of some mythical enemy. His was a bad case of persecution mania, which worsened during the hours of darkness.

That night the Chief entered the critical phase of his illness. He uttered long, rattling coughs and began to pick at the blankets and coverlets wrapping him. Observers were the more surprised the following morning when the sun rose to reveal, not a corpse, but a man struggling, with all the fury of a cross child, to maintain his hold upon life.

Someone stripped off the tarpaulin in which Chris was wrapped. He huddled closer to the floorboards. Alarming sounds dinned in his ears. First he realised it was raining: a fine drizzle, not the furious downpour it seemed when his covering was so rudely removed. (In that instant it had assumed the nightmare appearance of a tidal wave!) Then there was the heavy, ear-splitting noise of the unmuffled motor. Finally someone called his name. He realised this had been going on for some time.

"Chris! Chris! *Chris!*"

He did not reply at once: partly from self-protection, also because he had an aversion to the abbreviation of his Christian name. This was not due to superstition. He was unsure why. Perhaps just a matter of taste?

"Chris, can't you hear me? *Chris!*"

"What is it?"

"At last! We're out of luck, chum. It's raining."

"So what?"

"So it's raining. Still, that's not too bad really. You'll just have to go more carefully than usual. Maybe you'll skid in the mud a bit, but that's all, Chris—don't worry——"

Christopher felt the presence overhead. The fellow panted as though in the throes of sexual intercourse. "He's scared," Chris thought. "He's wrong to be scared. Fear is the worst thing that can happen to anybody. He must think one hell of a lot of me to run the risk of getting into real trouble every time. If I take a tumble and break my neck, it'll mean a few years in quod for this pal of mine—not to mention his boss."

This thought recurred at critical moments.

"Come on now, Chris. We're nearly there. Listen carefully: you've to get this straight. Last time the boss heard a noise he asked me afterwards what had happened. Had something fallen off? So this time I'm going to sling your case right into the bush. If I drop it on the road there'll be a clatter and the boss is bound to hear it. He'd probably stop, too, if I know him. So the bush it's to be. Doesn't make any difference really, but we must be careful, see?"

"Oh, don't worry about my case, chum; it's on its last legs, anyway."

"Still, it *is* your case, isn't it? Must have cost you a packet when you bought it."

"I forget," Chris said.

The heavy breathing continued. Christopher thought: "The trouble with this chap is, you always need explanations, endless infernal nattering!"

"Get ready now," the other man told him, rather nervously. "We're almost at the spot. Come right out from under that tarpaulin—there, that's right. Watch that rail, it's pretty slippery. Hang on tight. You've really the knack of it now. You ought to, after the practice—Christ! Stay where you are for a minute—no, for God's sake, Chris, don't go any lower! You oughtn't to fool around like that, even if you don't know what giddiness means. Wait till he's changed down into second before you jump —you're bound to slip a bit, but for Pete's sake don't fall upon your face. Try to balance, spread your arms out as though you were being crucified. Oh the old bastard! He'd never drive in anything but fourth if he could manage it. Wouldn't be difficult with the load we're humping today, either: three-bags-full of sweet damn-all. God, why doesn't he—— Ah, at last! There he goes into third —wait a bit longer—second now—*go*!!"

Far from slipping, Christopher landed squarely upon his feet, arms outstretched and weaving. The truck was slowed almost to walking pace. His posture resembled a punch-drunk boxer, sagging back against the ropes to avoid passing out. Then he hopped nimbly up the bank, retrieved his suitcase and jumped back on to the road. The truck laboured uphill in first, slipping on the mud surface. Christopher pursued it, drew abreast, gripped the out-stretched hand of his friend, the driver's mate. The latter had half-retreated under the tarpaulin to shelter from the rain. Chris ran beside the truck, laughing and talking, holding his friend's hand until the driver accelerated again. Chris had to let go. Despite the rain, he stood waving till a bend in the road took the truck out of sight.

The English master at Chris's college had spent a good deal of that school year discussing the Exotic. He claimed it was what you found, or expected to find, at the journey's end. Chris looked forward to quite a few things on returning to his home village, but none seemed the least exotic. The worst that could happen—especially when picking up old threads—was fear.

To be afraid and not know of what.

Every house was bolted except that belonging to one old woman, probably the oldest in the place. This village was supposed to lie under curse of the *Bilig* (evil demons). Certainly it contained a remarkable number of sinister old hags. Grandma, as she was called in the village, brightened up upon seeing Chris, opened her mouth in a toothless grin that would have scared anyone else into a fit.

"Well, boy," she said, with a feeble cackle, "you've finished with your studies for good now, eh?"

54

"No, Grandma—just on holiday, same as before."

"Same as before—you said it, not me, boy! That's a question between you and your mother, anyway. How long have you this time?"

"Two and a half months, Grandma. Seventy-five whole days!"

"That's an awful lot, boy. You must be pleased, eh? I suppose you've just arrived. You look as though you've just strolled over from the next village—on foot, too! Did you catch the bus, though?"

"No such luck, Grandma. Flat broke. Not a sou. I managed to hitch a lift with a truck-driver I know."

"Just like you," the old woman said, cheerfully. "Typical! You know, I was talking about you only the other day, to your mother——"

"I bet I know what you said, too."

"I said you were the only one of her three sons who knew how to get himself out of a jam. It's true, too, boy."

After endless compliments of this sort, Grandma announced that if he wanted to see his folks right away, he only had to slip up to the new fields; those that had just been cleared. The whole village was there, burning the scrub—a bit too early, in Grandma's estimate—but she had avoided going herself. She admitted, though, that the recent touch of rain might mean frequent showers during the next few days. When she offered him food, Chris havered a while before refusing. He was horribly hungry, but being fresh from college had certain qualms about Grandma's lax notions of hygiene. He excused himself on the grounds of being anxious to see his family.

"How big you're getting nowadays," Grandma said, admiringly. There were tears in her eyes. "If only your poor father were alive today, just so as he could see what a huge great chap you are! He was so fond of you always, you know." She paused, adding: "You must be pretty strong too, boy, eh?"

"Oh, I get by."

"Maybe you could come and give me a hand in my patch some time? Just once or twice? I'm so old, you see, I haven't any strength left. You will come, boy, won't you?"

"Sure I will, Grandma. I'll help you out—as I've always done. I'd start tomorrow if it wasn't Sunday. I'll be over Monday, Grandma."

A voice behind him said, abruptly: "You've to leave for Essazam, Chris, right away, since you're here on the spot. I was going to send Ntolo, but you were the one your poor aunt brought up. Seeing you're available and she's having some trouble——"

It was neither a friendly nor hostile voice. Its intonations reminded Chris of a young girl, just become a mother, but unsure what it was all about. Nervous, light-pitched almost to the point of reediness, it aroused no compassion. Chris had recently come to realise that pity was something which people could exist without. They were capable of coming through the crises unaided. His coolness surprised him. He kept his back to the road, remaining there in the position adopted for his chat with Grandma. He showed no immediate inclination to turn round and face his mother.

Now that his pity for her had gone, the only remaining emotion was filial love. He had no idea how to make contact with her. Ever since the day when, as quite a young woman, she had first been alone with her "horde of brats" —in reality four!—she had suffered from chronic fears; a terror of life.

Chris had not seen her arrival. She was right there behind him. Where was Grigri? Chris leant further forward, elbows firmly planted upon Grandma's window-sill, waiting for his kid sister to hurl herself at him. Every time he returned this was the moment he began to feel happy again—waiting for Grigri's whirlwind greeting. This time he seemed likely to encounter disappointment. As he grew older he realised he was becoming increasingly involved with Grigri and indifferent to Mama.

Mama still behaved like a half-wit, her voice stubborn. She would prevent anyone answering back, if it killed her. Herself a weak character, she was scared of her children. She knew all of them, Chris and Ntolo in particular, were inclined to dispute her authority.

Finally Chris turned. While she talked, he examined her at leisure. She had a thin face, her cheeks being very attractively decorated with fine tattoo-marks, like indelible pencil-lines. Her expression was frank. She looked people straight in the eye, with brave resignation. Like certain domestic animals, she had become dull-witted through following a repetitive daily routine. Chris was amazed that she still carried herself like a girl, despite the huge basket slung upon her back, crammed to bursting-point with provisions. Chris's practised eye recognised a porcupine's tail.

"Heavens!" he exclaimed, with faintly malicious admiration. "A porcupine, no less! Who have we to thank for this tit-bit?"

"Your brother Ntolo. He's not like you, wasting time polishing school benches with the seat of his pants, playing at being a kid—he really *does* something!"

"Well, well, Mama. Is that your welcoming hullo? I can see we're going to have a high old party this evening, Grandma—better join in. You'll never regret it. I'm inviting you personally."

"But *Chris*, you stupid boy," said his mother, "I keep telling you, you've to start for Essazam, right away——"

"What the hell is all this Essazam business, Mama? Who's put a curse upon whom? I suppose it *is* a curse——"

"Yes, yes, it's a curse, right enough," his mother sighed. "Can you imagine it? That drunken, polygamous old pig

57

—your aunt's husband—that is, I mean, the Chief——"

"I get your meaning, Mama. What's he been up to?"

"He's dead. He's passed over. It seems there wasn't even time to baptise him."

"How did it happen? An accident?"

"Not likely! He fell sick and died in his bed. Only two or three days from start to finish. It'd have been another matter if anyone in Essazam had thought of baptising him. You've to go there right away, Chris. These Essazam folk aren't like us. They're backward savages. If I know them, they're probably knocking hell out of the lecherous old swine's widows at this very moment. They'll say it's because one of the wretched women did away with him. You've to go and protect your aunt, Chris."

Chris was momentarily taken aback. He made a fine show of stubborn recalcitrance.

"After all," he argued, "it's Melig who's really qualified to deal with this sort of thing. He's the eldest, isn't he? You've told me often enough he's stepped into Papa's shoes; he should be sent to Essazam. I'll lay any money you like you haven't been able to find your precious eldest son anywhere, Mama. Isn't that so, eh? He's a dirty-minded, lecherous puppy and probably sniffing up some bitch's arse at this very minute——"

"Don't insult your elders, Chris——"

"Oh no? You've just insulted a dead man, haven't you?"

"Perhaps I have, but that doesn't give you the right to talk like that about Melig. Your duty is to venerate him as you would your father——"

"Who the hell said so?" Chris enquired. He was laughing helplessly by now, beating his clenched fists against his thighs: not over his mother's stupidity but in delight at Grigri's arrival. She flung herself at him helter-skelter and was hugging him in a tight embrace.

"Who said so?" repeated Mama doggedly. Her persistence was quite astonishing. "Why, it's a commandment handed down by our ancestors. That was the way *they* behaved——"

"And I suppose their conduct was invariably impeccable, huh?" Chris mocked. "One of the reasons I've always had respect for polygamy is that our ancestors handed it down to us——"

"Don't get me into a temper, Chris," Mama shouted. "I'm too tired to argue."

Chris laughed harder than ever. His little sister hugged him with frenzied violence. He caught her up at arms' length, whirling her twice round his head. The third time he had to put her down. She had grown fast and was too heavy for Chris. At this time—that is, July 1948—he was undernourished. Almost a starving schoolboy.

They were joined by Ntolo, amiable as always, and festooned with the authentic gear of a peasant, bill-hook, chopper, spear. Together they trooped homewards, arguing fiercely as they went. This kind of family row was a longstanding passion with them all.

"Chris, you're forgetting your case," Grandma shouted.

Chris either did not or would not understand. "Look, Grandma," he called back, "I've to leave right away for Essazam, I'm told. That means I won't be able to help you till I get back. See?"

Finally Ntolo retraced his steps, rescuing Chris's case.

When they were home, and Mama had finished fussing about unlocking the padlocked front door, battle commenced in earnest. It was Grigri who fired the first shot.

"What's happened, Chris?" the little girl asked. "Mama came and told us that you'd been expelled from school."

"Wrong, ducky. They just took away my living-in allowance." He explained the difference, succinctly.

"What had you done? Mama said you hit a White teacher. Is that true?"

"For heaven's sake, ducky; you know how Mama

59

exaggerates! Even if I'd wanted to bash this chap's face, I couldn't. Honestly, Grigri, you ought to see him! He's as tall as a baobab tree and wide as—as—well, *that* wide. I certainly didn't hit him, love, I hardly even *argued* with him——"

"But you did," Mama interrupted, "and very rudely, too. You've never known how to speak to respectable people. I'm telling you, Chris, if you don't mend your ways you'll suffer far worse. Look: did you or did you not address him in such a way that everyone thought you were going to strike him? Yes or no?"

"So he *didn't* do it," Grigri said, in a very disappointed voice. She was wondering why Mama had lied.

"Shut up, you," Mama told her sharply.

"So she's not even allowed to open her mouth now, eh?" enquired Chris, painfully surprised. " 'Shut up', is it? What next?"

This gave Grigri (no less stubborn than Mama) exactly the encouragement she needed.

"How did you manage to live, then, Chris?" she asked. "Where did you sleep? What did you do about food?"

"I'm surprised Mama didn't tell you the ghastly details on her return!"

The child pulled a rude face. "Oh, her! I don't believe a word of what she says these days. She came home and said you were starving to death. You weren't *really* starving, were you, Chris?"

Touched, the boy suddenly realised these questions had worried his sister—for weeks, even months. He threw out his chest, roared with laughter, and strode to and fro across the room, declaiming in a loud, artificial voice.

"Look at me, Grigri! Look well at your big brother! Am I the kind of man who'd be likely to die of starvation? I'm not, am I? So don't ever worry on my account, Grigri. Just forget it."

Abandoning his little comedy, his voice edged with

quiet anger, he recounted what actually had happened, the injustice he had endured. He sounded doomed by some inexorable curse to find the wrong side of everyone he met. What *had* he done to annoy this physical training instructor? Nothing, save to say that he felt exhausted on this particular morning. Chris did not make a habit of this excuse. Claiming to be incapable of climbing the rope, an exercise favoured by the instructor, he was given an unceremonious kick in the backside.

"My God, it wasn't that I didn't want to take a poke at him," Chris said. "Think of the hammering he'd have given me, if I had! He could have pounded me into a jelly with his right hand tied behind his back."

A scandalous parody of a Court of Discipline was then held. Chris was deprived of his boarding-rights without being allowed any defence. He found refuge with acquaintances in the southern suburb of the town. There Mama had visited him. As his boarding-fees were automatically stopped ("Knew what they were doing, didn't they, the bastards?") he had to re-arrange his day. In the morning he attended lectures. He sat up late at night reading or composing essays. During the afternoon he did all sorts of odd jobs to make a little money. He did not jib at laundry-work, which included washing women's smalls.

The family watched him intently during this recital of woes. They observed how even the recollection first heated him mildly, then led him, through stages of exasperation, to fury. His hands clenched, as though strangling an enemy. His voice shook. He blinked rapidly, bared his large square teeth in a kind of nervous snarl, flecks of foam gathering at the corners of his mouth.

Grigri burst into tears.

"Well done!" declared Mama ironically. Her notions were somewhat old-fashioned. "Well done indeed! Why couldn't you learn how to behave properly? It's very decent of these White folk to trouble over you. They're doing the teaching, aren't they, not you? Very well, then! Stop giving them impertinent back-chat. Treat them with proper respect. Learn a few manners, that's all."

"Oh be quiet, Mama!" Ntolo burst out, too exasperated for restraint. "You don't know what you're talking about! You never went to school."

Then Ntolo, normally taciturn, rounded upon Chris. "Well anyway, I hope you'll drop all this education nonsense now. It's not so bad—you've your first diploma, haven't you?"

"Ah for God's sake," Chris said, "don't start that crap again, *mon vieux*." Hardly noticing what he was doing, he found himself switching into French. "I'm not going to chuck my hand in with only a year to my *baccalauréat*. Make no mistake about that. Why do you suppose I nearly killed myself to get the Intermediate? I'm in for my Finals this year, boy; top grade. What's more, I've done so well, I'll almost certainly have my grant and boarding-rights restored. Never give up, that's the secret of success. Stick at it, lad, stick at it!"

"Yes, yes, I won't argue with you about *that*," Ntolo said, sour, resigned. He too spoke French. "Go on, do what you like. You always have. You're not going to change overnight. *I'm* not the person to be giving you good advice. I'm an old lag myself by now, as they say."

"Come off it, boy; stop talking like a c—t."

"Oh Lordy," gasped Mama. "*What* was that you said?"

"Don't worry, Mama," Chris said, sadly and wearily. "I wasn't referring to you."

He hated arguing with Ntolo. Yet it was hard to relinquish any of his *idées fixes*. To win his *baccalauréat* amounted to an obsession. The boys were half-brothers. Moreover, Ntolo's mother had died at his birth, a tragedy with one fortunate result: Papa's reconciliation with Father Van Hout. After Papa's second marriage the priest constantly referred to him by all manner of derogatory epithets: polygamist, savage, apostate, renegade, false Christian and even more extravagant terms.

Chris looked dismally round the house. It was slowly falling to pieces. There were large gaps in the puddled clay walls which no one had bothered to repair. Bare wattle was visible beneath. Some of the shutters had come away from the windows. They were replaced at night with anything handy. He shook his head despairingly at Ntolo.

"But look, I can't do everything at once, Chris! I've to work in what's left of the cocoa-plantation. Help Mama in the fields. I let that sort of thing slide. I know, I know, it's wrong of me to be a stick-in-the-mud. I ought to be energetic and go-ahead, like the rest of the world——"

"You know damn well it's not you I'm getting at," Chris said, his patience snapping. "You need someone to make your plans for you. It was our dear brother I was thinking of. Still, if Papa hadn't left us this shack, where the hell would we be today? Poor old Papa! You'd have a fit if you could see what's become of the old home now. God, what a crumbling ruin! There'll be damn-all left soon. Just the corrugated iron on the roof."

Mama had disappeared into the poky little room that did duty as a kitchen. Gathering her eldest son was under discussion, she shot out again, planting herself aggressively among her brood.

"Who were you talking about just now?" she snapped, daring them to tell her. "Well, haven't any of you the courage to own up? Call yourselves *men*!"

"Listen, Mama," Chris said, "just wrap up and leave us in peace, will you? We weren't discussing *him*"—this piece of lying effrontery slipped out without effort—"we don't wish *him* any harm; we venerate him as though he were our father——"

Their eldest brother's thunderous voice suddenly could be heard outside, shouting for Grigri.

63

"Agri!" he roared. "Agri! *Agri!* Go and fetch some water from the well! Come on, hurry up, off with you to draw me a bucketful or two—I want a good hot bath. Christ, I hate to think of the amount of liquor I put away last night. Drinking until the small hours! Mad, quite mad. Agri! Come *on*!"

He entered the house, suddenly seeing Chris. He choked. A large part of his speech remained unuttered. He made himself very small and slunk across the room—almost noiselessly, for him. He lowered himself carefully into a rickety chair in the darkest corner. Seeing her eldest son tip-toeing about so, tail between his legs, Mama appeared mortified. In a voice shaking with fury, she said: "Did you hear what you were told to do, Agri?"

The girl made a pretence of rising. Her face bore a characteristic expression. A private mocking grin, speaking volumes. It hinted she was aware just how Chris's arrival had shifted the balance of power. Chris, who knew these thoughts before his sister uttered a word, now said to her: "Grigri, my poppet, sit down and relax. Make yourself comfortable. So we're to go off to the well and draw water for this fine gentleman's bath, are we? I'd like to see it."

The girl did not crow over victory. She returned calmly to her place and sat down again. They all remained silent for one awful moment during which storm-clouds gathered and thickened. They sat, avoiding each other's eyes, feigning ignorance of the canker gnawing at their hearts; a family divided against itself. Ntolo sat in his corner, looking even lonelier and more exhausted. Perhaps his extra-sensitive nature foresaw tragedy to come.

Suddenly Chris rose, unable to stand the atmosphere. He exploded like a time-bomb with a delayed fuse. Knowing him well, Ntolo felt terribly sorry for him. He realised that Chris was finding it well-nigh impossible to control his emotions. The difficulties of the previous nine months had shaken him up badly.

A row of quite terrifying violence ensued between Chris and Mama. Melig and the little girl sat trembling like banana-leaves in a tornado. Chris was very tall and thin. He seemed bigger at the end of every school year, and loomed over them, angrier than they had ever seen him. Despite Mama's appearance of authority, assumed to bolster her shaky position, the whole family bowed before the onslaught of this irate schoolboy. Chris swore personally to "do" anyone treating his sister as a slave.

Then, since it was now fairly late in the day, he determined to set off for Essazam. He polished the blade of a big sheath-knife inherited from Papa. Chris did not know the first thing about using it! He swore that anyone annoying Grigri in his absence would have to explain to the sharp end of this lethal weapon. This said, he packed a small bundle of necessities. Since it was too late to catch a bus, he managed to squeeze twice the normal amount of cash out of Mama. He explained that it cost more to hitch-hike. The driver ran a risk of prosecution for carrying passengers illegally.

Chris in fact travelled on foot, keeping his money for more important needs. He left his village as evening was drawing in, striking straight into the forest, keeping on after dark, taking one short cut after another. He uprooted a length of sugar-cane from a field to slake his thirst. Later he picked and ate a quantity of bananas. It was after midnight when yet another short cut brought him out at a village whose inhabitants he knew well. Here he found a bed in an old woman's hut and slept till morning

The boy awoke with a start. Resentfully he rubbed his eyes, conscious of an indefinable malaise. Eyes fixed, expression unchanging, he sought to identify his trouble. He had certainly retired very late. He could not have had much sleep. Why, for heaven's sake, *had* he gone to bed so late? His youthful memory unfolded the long scene in retrospect; baptism and all. He felt anxious. He was unconvinced that there was any value in the ritual used by that madwoman when administering the sacrament. Would it have been potent enough, notwithstanding, to admit the Chief into Heaven?

The boy listened, ears attuned to the faintest sound. He feared aural confirmation of what he expected. Though he stood up in bed, craned his neck and peered through the window, he could not hear a single wailing woman, or catch the most distant mutter of tom-toms. There was no indication of the two missionaries' return. Why were they delayed? What could have happened to stop Le Guen celebrating Sunday Mass in his own Mission Church?

Come to that, what time was it? A queer Sunday, with no bell to toll or Mass to serve at. What sense had there been in decorating the altar if there was to be no service?

Being convinced the Chief was about to die, the boy had remained in the village till dawn, despite the cook's protests. The latter wanted to take him back to the Mission House.

He had sat up late, like the grown-ups, listening, watching, carefully memorising every incident and interesting item of conversation, with which to delight Le Guen on his return. About the time the partridges had begun to call, in the very early morning, the grown-ups had settled down for a snooze in their usual uncomfortable postures. Some propped their backs against the wall, or dozed off upon their feet. At this point the boy had left, stumbling and swaying with sheer fatigue, brought to the point of tears by so many emotional experiences. He made his way back alone through the half-dark. Reaching the Mission House, he fell asleep the moment his head touched the pillow.

"How am I going to spend my Sunday?" the boy asked

himself, anxiously. It was not that, at his age, he was in a rut. The unprecedented circumstances, however, had affected daily life. The "normal" no longer applied.

Though serious and thoughtful he was practical enough on occasion, impulsive when a quick decision was called for. Then he seldom paused to weigh up the ideas racing through his mind. Until now his selections had been lucky. Le Guen spoke not of the boy's impulsiveness so much as of his 'intuition', 'instinct' and 'flair'. Complimentary terms indeed. As Le Guen said, such praise might go to the boy's head. It also suggested the kind of adult he might become.

He was hardly up before running into an argument with his friend the cook. Caught at a most inopportune moment, he was executing a complicated series of acrobatic movements that ended by landing him astride the enormous Mission bicycle. Frequently error occurred and he found himself standing instead upon the cross-bar!

"Hullo-ullo there!" sang out the cook, in a powerful, well-nourished sounding voice. The boy's athletic activities ceased. He was breathing hard, ashamed and angry for any grown-up to have witnessed this struggle with the machine. He was uncomfortably aware that his antics were liable to arouse ridicule from adult onlookers, able to vault effortlessly into the saddle.

"Well, well, well, little man." The cook's tones were bantering. "And where might you be off to in such a hurry?"

"I've permission to ride the thing, haven't I?" the boy grumbled. He wondered if the cook wanted revenge for having had to return alone to the Mission the previous night. A superstitious man, scared stiff of the dark. "I've been authorised to use this bicycle," the boy repeated.

"You quite sure, chum?" with a sardonic laugh.

"Yes I am," the boy answered vehemently. "Father Le

67

Guen told me I could, the day he left. All he said about it was that I mustn't damage it."

"I don't understand it at all." The cook tried to look worried, not really succeeding. "I just don't get it. They left—let's see now—on Tuesday. That makes nearly a week you've had every opportunity to ride this bicycle. Until today you didn't touch the thing. And now——"

"The Chief was ill," pleaded the boy.

"And now maybe he's better again?"

"Are you just trying to annoy me, or did you mean that seriously?"

"There's just one thing you forget, kiddo. I'm the bloke who's responsible for you here at the Mission, especially when we're left alone together. I don't mind your going for a ride. But have you any idea what time it is? Half-past eleven, you thickhead! Who's going to ring the Angelus with our high and mighty Gustave busy breaking speed records along the main road?"

"Couldn't you do it for me?"

"No, I couldn't and that's flat."

"I'll walk back to the Mission with you tomorrow night——"

"Come off it! Think I'm scared, or something? The very idea!"

"Please, just as a favour for me, then——"

"No, no, no. Everyone ought to stick to his own job." With that the cook gave Gustave a cheerful slap on the bottom, picked him up, set him in the saddle and pushed the bicycle down the track, saying: "Don't count on me to ring the Angelus for you, so you'd better be back in good time."

Less than a mile from the Mission the boy wheeled round. This mid-day bell-ringing business was aggravatingly upon his mind. He ached to be off. When he was back, he went and looked at the clock. Still only twenty

68

to twelve! Never mind, he told himself, it cannot be a mortal sin to ring the Angelus twenty minutes early.

He approached the bell-rope, hesitated a moment or two, then, biting his lip, grasped the rope and tugged it smartly several times. This done, he quickly scrambled back on to the bicycle (with the aid of a handy post) and shot off again without looking back. Somewhere behind him the cook roared furiously. It sounded like a chimpanzee being burnt alive.

The boy felt cheerful and relieved. At least he *had* rung the mid-day bell, even if early and sketchily. He cycled out on to the main road, and pedalled away for dear life.

A considerable way off Le Guen and Schloegel bent over Lizzie's engine. The wretched van looked more harassed, exhausted and generally worn out than ever.

"Well, Your Reverence," Schloegel said, "I'll have another go; but it's only to clear my conscience, if you get me."

He streamed with sweat. For another ten minutes Le Guen watched him wrestle with the starting-handle, straightening up at intervals to get his breath back, hoisting up the sleeves and skirts of his soutane. Finally he stripped off the offending garment. Abandoning his efforts, he shook his head in playful despair.

"Nothing to be done with her today. The lady's on strike, blast her eyes! You know the countryside well, don't you, Your Reverence?"

"Like the back of my hand, heaven help me."

"How far along the Mission road are we, do you suppose?"

"We're something like ten miles from Essazam. Maybe a bit more; certainly not less. There's bound to be a milestone near."

"Fair enough," Schloegel agreed. "You've got this bush all worked out, I see."

"The nearest village—a tiny hamlet, really—is about

a couple of miles away. I once gave the Last Sacraments to an old woman there. Tough old bird she was, too." Le Guen changed his tone to one of mock-melodrama. "Lost in the heart of the African jungle!" Reverting to normal, he added: "On a weekday we shouldn't have had to wait long before some truck-driver picked us up. Today there's no traffic on the roads."

"No? And why not?"

"It's the Sabbath, Brother Joseph. Remember?"

"Have you noticed something odd? Amazing how many Christians are around when it's a matter of not working!"

"I'm thirsty," said Le Guen. "What about you?"

They sat down again, side by side, on the wooden bench serving as front seat. After a little rummaging underneath, Schloegel produced a gourd.

"Well, that's all we've got. A pint or two of cheap *vino*. You have first swig, Your Reverence."

Each in turn put the neck of the gourd to his mouth and swallowed some wine, smacking his lips as the after-taste hit him.

"The Bishop's wine isn't exactly what you might call *fresh*," Schloegel observed.

"No, it isn't!"

Schloegel began some exceedingly disrespectful, even blasphemous observations upon their late host's way of life, in particular his arrogance and ostentation. After a little of this Le Guen suddenly recalled the esteem in which good priests always should hold their Bishop. So he sought to divert the conversation. His eye lit upon a roadside bush. This behaved in the oddest manner, quivering like a lazy heifer, half asleep in the sun and bothered by flies. Presently a huge lout of a man emerged, grinning from ear to ear, naked except for a filthy ragged scrap (which conceivably might once have been a pair of khaki shorts) wound sketchily about his buttocks and private parts. He waved a cross-bow in his right hand and had a machete pressed under his left arm-pit. Hastily changing the cross-bow to the other hand, his right arm was unencumbered for the ceremony about to be performed.

Superbly self-assured, he walked up to the two missionaries and regally offered them his gigantic paw. Their small frail hands were enveloped. All three of them became intimate friends of long standing. The scene resembled a corny explorer's story.

"I heard your van stop," the man said, grinning happily. "I was busy hunting just then." In a vague sort of way, his wave embraced the entire forest with a self-satisfied landowner's air.

"It's tough going, you know. Very tough at this time of year. You know what we need now? A nice drop of rain. Just the job."

"What's he on about?" Schloegel asked. Never having been called upon to make Essazam converts he knew little of their dialect.

"Nothing very much," Le Guen answered. "He seems chatty for a hunter, though. Here the rains aren't early enough to suit him. You'd hear a different story from the women in the fields. It's eternal opposition, you know. Hunter versus farmer; man against woman——"

Tired of standing on ceremony, the hunter launched upon a long, detailed account of the jungle fauna and their strange habits. His remarks were interspersed with laughter and excited cries. All the animals were reviewed: monkeys, antelopes, porcupines and salamanders. He showed a connoisseur's appreciation not only of their intelligence—according to him, superior to that of man—but also of their infinite cunning. Then he said, irrelevantly: "Looks as if the van won't go any more. What's the matter?"

"A break-down," Le Guen explained.

"Well that *is* a nuisance, isn't it?" the man was duly

71

sympathetic. "Especially as there won't be a single truck through today. You may be stranded quite a time, you know. Maybe you would like some bananas? Horrible things, *I* think. Last time I tried them I got a dose of worms. You townsfolk love 'em, I'm told."

"He's offering us bananas," Le Guen told Schloegel.

"Just the thing." Schloegel rubbed his hands.

"Bring us your bananas," Le Guen instructed. "You know, you're a fine fellow."

The hunter blushed under his black skin. "I'm afraid I can't do that, Father. You'll have to look for them yourself. I shan't be near the road again. I've lost too much time already. Melingui probably will have given me the slip meanwhile."

"Melingui?" queried Le Guen, uneasily.

"That's right: she's the monkey I've been stalking— for two days now. I've lived in the jungle, alone with Melingui, the little bitch. You couldn't catch her off guard. There wasn't one moment when I could draw a bead on her with the remotest chance of hitting her. I call her Melingui because I'm obviously dealing with a female monkey. She's a magnificent specimen, whatever her sex. As I was telling you. I've been after her for days, but she's up to every trick—camouflage, dodging back on her tracks. Anything to shake me off. Oh, I know very well I'll beat her in the end. It's all a matter of practice, you know. For the moment, you might say, she calls the tune." And he roared with laughter.

"He says we've got to go and look for the bananas ourselves," Le Guen told his companion. "He can't return to the road. He's lost too much time already."

"Why? Is his business as urgent as all that? Know what I think, Your Reverence? I don't believe a word this chap says!"

"No, no, Brother Joseph, you're wrong there. I'll go

with him." He told the hunter in dialect: "I'm coming with you. He'll stay and guard the van."

They were hardly into the bush before the hunter said confidentially: "So he was scared, eh?"

"*Scared?* What of? For heaven's sake, what are you trying to hint?"

"He's an odd chap," the hunter insisted. "He can't speak our dialect. To look at him I'd say he's been quite a while in the country. I'm pretty sure I know who he is. You're going to visit the Mission at Essazam, aren't you?"

"We *are* the Essazam missionaries."

"Ah, I understand now. I'm afraid I don't belong to your religion, so I couldn't tell at first. All the same, I'm sure I recognise the other fellow—he's Brother Cho—, Jo—, oh, I don't know how you pronounce it; I never went to school."

"Yes, that is he."

"He built the Chief's Palace, didn't he?"

"You know all about him, don't you?"

"Talking about the Chief," the hunter brushed aside tall grasses and overhanging boughs as he strode majestically along, "I can't think why you're away from Essazam at the time of the old boy's death. I always heard you two were his greatest friends."

Le Guen listened in consternation. The hunter unhurriedly recounted the various phases of the Chief's illness, winding up that the old fellow was in his final agony. At any moment he would pass away. The missionary might expect to hear tom-toms spreading the message of death. Yes, perhaps before returning to the truck.

"As for Brother Joseph. I know him, all right. I watched him at work when the poor Chief's Palace was under construction. He certainly had plenty of energy. There's no doubt the tribe's going to suffer great loss. There was a ring round the moon the other day, you know. Besides, you've only got to watch Melingui. Animals never mistake

73

such things. You know, Father, the worst of all is uncertainty. Judging by the speed with which the disease knocked him out, the Chief should have been dead long ago. In the normal course of events, that is. The fever couldn't make up its mind one way or the other. Everyone waits to see what happens. Accordingly the whole place is in suspense. Don't mistake me, I wish him no harm. He was as close as a brother, even though he was the Chief. We really *ought* to know whether he's to live or die!"

The hunter abandoned the path and swung into the thick bush, taking little further notice of Le Guen. The latter had great difficulty in following. Tall grasses and tangled branches continually tripped him up. They whipped across his face, half-blinding him. He lost sight of the hunter altogether for an uncomfortable moment. He was making up his mind to call him when they became reunited. The Negro was placidly slashing at a banana tree. One machete cut severed an entire stem.

Le Guen said: "Listen, my friend. What you told me is true, isn't it? You really mean the Chief is dying?"

"Certainly I do, Father. You ought to hurry back to the Mission as fast as you can. Who knows, you might still be in time to baptise him. Who can swear he won't stand in need of holy water once he has crossed to the other side?"

"I hardly think so," Le Guen said.

Joseph Schloegel sighed with relief when he saw his companion reappear. Le Guen was breathless and streaming with sweat. His long beard was full of leaves and other vegetable matter; his shoes clogged with grey mud. Every few yards he rested. He dragged an enormous stem of bananas, possibly heavier than the Cross at Golgotha.

With Schloegel's assistance, he just managed to hoist this load into the back of the van.

"Oh, the swine!" Le Guen panted. "He dropped me like a piece of stinking fish, when it suited him. 'That's all

74

yours, Father,' he told me, pointing at the bananas. And then—presto!—he vanished! Into thin air!''

The two men sat again on the wooden bench. They began eating the few bananas that had fallen off the stem. Far away down the road before them appeared a tiny black dot. It grew as they watched, soon recognisable as a human perched upon an enormous bicycle. The rider seemed to be performing a kind of crazy monkey's-dance on this odd machine.

Le Guen ventured the opinion that it was a frog.

"Not a bit of it," said Schloegel, determined to outdo him. "Not a bit of it! This is a unique species."

The phenomenon bowled along at a quite fantastic speed. They were used to Lizzie's tortoise-crawl.

"But—so *that's* it!" Le Guen murmured, recognising Gustave. The hunter's story all came back to him.

"Lord, Lord, Lord," the priest repeated to himself, unable to analyse his feelings.

"What's the matter, Your Reverence? Aren't you feeling well?" Schloegel was seriously worried.

"Gustave," Le Guen whispered. "It's Gustave!"

Flabbergasted, they stared at the nightmare figure approaching. Despite his dizzy speed, he had the appearance of the boy they knew. They watched him halt beside the van. In order to alight the boy had to tilt the bicycle. Le Guen opened the van door and hastened to assist. Gustave was panting dangerously. Great drops of sweat were pearled on his forehead and streaming down his cheeks. His veins had become unnaturally swollen by the gigantic effort he had just made. They stood out on every visible part of his body.

Le Guen grasped his hand, asking if the Chief were dead. A futile question, the priest realised. If it had happened, a hundred miles of surrounding countryside would have learnt the news. Gustave, always patient with Le Guen, replied that the Chief was not dead yet, but that it was only a matter of time. In graphic detail he described the baptism by Yosifa, astonished by Le Guen's approval.

"A blessing, indeed, that he found one Christian soul to aid him! I thank you, Lord!"

Le Guen then hopped on to the discarded bicycle and pedalled hard for Essazam.

Brother Joseph watched this scene in astonishment, not understanding its purport. Being neither a mystic nor an intellectual, he habitually took practical action when faced by problems beyond his imagination. There were people in Essazam who declared that Brother Joseph was not a man of God in the Le Guen sense. This Bantu judgment cast doubt upon Schloegel's chastity. Yet for all his solid physique, Brother Joseph was both a humble and a modest man. Furthermore he was excellent company and trod lightly for his fifty-odd years.

He comforted himself, reflecting that the Bishop had allotted them sufficient funds to continue the work of building a permanent church in Essazam. He rubbed his hands in high-minded anticipation. Soon, perhaps tomorrow, he might be on the job.

Some way off Chris hurried along. He had just emerged from the forest and was impatiently reckoning up the number of bends before the next short cut. The sun literally roasted the surface of the road. He walked on the grassy verge, where it was cooler, thanks to rows of palm-trees flanking the route. Their wide-leafed branches created a shady corridor. As he approached the last turning before the track he was so zealously seeking, Chris sighed with relief, quickening his pace. As he was about to turn off the main road, he saw a distant shabby and very stationary truck. He stopped to consider the implications.

He decided to stay on the road until he approached the truck. He strolled along in a casual, inoffensive sort of way, trying to whistle a tune, and doing his best to look the smart, cheerful, obliging fellow, eager to scrape acquaintance with a fellow-traveller. He thought Schloegel's grey beard highly comic but refrained from smiling, being so determined upon creating a favourable impression. He walked a little past Lizzie, turned back and touching his beret respectfully, said: "Praise be to God, Father!"

Schloegel acknowledged Chris's overture amiably enough. In this he differed from the majority of missionaries. They tended to be curt with such adventurous souls. Despite his reception, Chris kept walking, casually indifferent. Fifty yards from the truck, careful to remain in sight of its occupants, he climbed atop the small bank above the ditch; sat swinging his legs and mopping his forehead. His expression (it came quite naturally) was of a stoic simpleton. He racked his brains for some line of approach. Was he so grown up that he could not play a harmless joke on a half-witted *curé*?

Suddenly Chris recognised the face he had glimpsed peering out of the van. He bit his lip in surprise, thinking hard. It was indeed that bastard Joseph Schloegel's ugly mug! What in hell was he up to, sitting around like a village idiot? Who was he anyway, the little squirt? Just a jumped-up house-boy, a nobody! Chris had seen enough of Schloegel in Mission schooldays. A maniac for work, only stopped to eat or to play pranks with lady parishioners. Not that *he'd* found *that* difficult, being a well-built sort of chap. "Hell," Chris thought, "and I actually called him 'Father'! I suppose he was flattered."

It was Gustave who first spotted the young man's stratagem. Chris aroused his worst suspicions. The boy glanced at the missionary several times to learn, from Schloegel's expression, what he made of so odd a character. Completely unruffled, the old man watched Chris without hostility.

This young fellow looked a town-dweller. Obviously

he did not go to weekly confession like Gustave. The boy particularly disliked this kind of city slicker, with his over-brief, over-starched, too-well-ironed shorts; his rainbow shirt—its coloured squares glaring in the sunlight—and, final abomination, multi-coloured socks. The fellow sat, nonchalantly whistling and unlacing his canvas shoes. This done, he peeled off his socks to air his feet.

He sprang to his feet like a jack-in-the-box; grabbed a handy long stick. Howling wildly he slashed at a small lemon-tree beside the road.

"What on earth's got into him?" wondered Schloegel, more amused than perturbed.

"Probably a snake," Gustave said, delighted that this unpleasant person was on the defensive.

Schloegel leapt from the truck and went chivalrously to Chris's assistance. The latter, trembling with fright and anger, crouched over the lemon-bush, stick upraised. He peered unsuccessfully for his adversary.

"Oh, the horrible little beast!" Chris growled in French. "The bloody little sod of a thing! He might easily have bitten me—lucky I spotted him in time. To think there are people who say snakes don't attack you unless provoked! I ask you, what did I do? I was sitting there peacefully minding my own business, without moving. It's true I was *whistling*, but I don't call that provocation——"

They poked and thrashed about diligently among the lemon-bushes, without results. The 'horrible little animal' eluded them—for a very good reason.

"Oh, the bastard!" Chris went on, talking as though he were among his College friends. "He'd have loved to sink his fangs into me. Nothing would have pleased him more——"

"Really?" Schloegel said.

"Oh yes, it's true: I caught him in the very act of

78

wriggling up between my legs. My God! If I hadn't spotted him when I did, I shouldn't be the same man now!"

"No?" Schloegel was studying this eloquent young man carefully. Obviously a city-boy, member of that new post-war species. He had heard a lot about them, but had little first-hand experience of their ways.

"So you wouldn't be the same man, eh?" he remarked. "What would you be then, laddie? White, I suppose?"

Whereupon he gave a huge laugh. Chris decided the affair was going well.

At this point Brother Joseph, with embarrassment, realised he might be making this College boy lose face by failing to recognise him. How could he be sure who the boy was? He had seen thousands of young Negroes in the street. Besides, as he declared, he was incapable of telling a Bantu brother and sister apart. So he said to Chris, abruptly: "Look, who exactly are you? Forgive my asking you so bluntly, but you speak our language remarkably well!"

Thought Chris: "He's taking the trouble to be polite. The New Look in race relations *is* catching on, my word! Even we Essazam country boys feel its backwash. Good! Let's cash in on it."

So he told Schloegel that he was on his way to Essazam itself. There his aunt—his mother's sister, that was—had just lost her husband, the Paramount Chief.

"Christ," he thought, "*what was the old number's name?* Damned if the bugger's going to spoil my chance of a lift! Twenty miles on this old crock's a mixed blessing. But now I've stopped to rest it'll be hell trying to walk again."

Brother Joseph told him to wait in the truck till some famous "Hero of Kufra" came to set the engine running again. Greatly relieved, Chris sat upon the bench beside Gustave, who told him that while the Chief might be in his death agony, he had not actually passed away.

79

"If you imagine I give a f—— about that, you damned little Mission flunkey," Chris thought, "you're making a great mistake. All I'm concerned with is my aunt. Your godalmighty Montezuma can go stuff himself."

Presently Raphael arrived. Without difficulty he got Lizzie's engine turning over again. They set off just before nightfall. Chris, slightly put out, sat in the back, wedged between the harmonium, the bicycle upon which the Hero of Kufra had arrived, and the gigantic stem of bananas the talkative hunter had given to Le Guen.

2

I T was with mixed feelings, mostly of curiosity, that the
inhabitants of Essazam greeted the missionary's return.
They had practically forgotten about him. They saw
him regularly enough to treat him as a member of their
community. His departures caused little comment. This
was rather different. They had waited so long for the
Chief's death that they had run through every known
picturesque ceremony and custom. They were bored and
willing to amuse themselves with anything, or anyone,
turning up. Much fun was found anticipating the nervous
irritability of Le Guen when he arrived. This condition
they believed to afflict every European. They drove themselves to achieve the impossible, even when the situation
was hopeless—as opinion had decided the Chief's illness
to be.

Le Guen's first task on reaching Essazam was to ad-
minister Extreme Unction to the sick man. This ratified
the baptismal ceremony, to Gustave's relief.

To perform the rite Le Guen had to traverse the larger
part of the village and pass before the Palace—where a
large crowd of near-naked Elders snoozed, propped-up
shoulder to shoulder.

"What's *he* up to in there?" Ndibidi demanded of his
fellow-patriarch Ondoua beside him.

"I see you know nothing of their religion," Ondoua
said, banteringly. "He's going to give the Chief what they
call 'communion'. Above all, he's going to anoint him with
an oil that comes from his own country. This oil is a kind

81

of passport to the hereafter, to make sure he's received there as befits a Chief. But the Christians claim that the stuff can cure people, too—make them healthy in this world as well as the next. I can tell you, without doubt, that Yosifa will collect a very great deal of credit for having thought of baptising the Chief——"

"And for having actually *done* it," added Ndibidi.

"I agree! Ezoum tried several times, you know. The Chief refused point-blank."

That afternoon Le Guen left again for Ongola on the motorcycle-sidecar combination of the Mission's. This time he went mostly by rough bush-tracks, which considerably shortened his journey. He reached town well before nightfall. Some little black boys playing in the street showed him the way to the address he wanted. This was the private house of any senior official who might be available on a Sunday. The house he found belonged to the Chief Regional Administrator, no less; but Le Guen only discovered this later. Monsieur Lequeux turned out to be a shrimp, wearing a pink carnation. He was extremely natty in his dress and toilet. As yet Le Guen had no idea of his enormous power and influence and was unimpressed. The Administrator possessed another characteristic: he pronounced his r's in an odd way, unrelated to any known accent. This also disturbed Le Guen a little. He was an old Africa hand and justly claimed experience of every shade of colour there.

"You have wasted very little time getting here from Essazam, Father," Lequeux said, in a thin, high voice.

"That is true, Monsieur. I have to tell you that the Paramount Chief of the Essazam tribe is dying. Chief Essomba Mendouga——"

"Yes, yes, Father, I understand. My God, it's a serious thing, this. What happened exactly? Why wasn't he taken to hospital? God, it really is serious——"

Le Guen recounted what had happened. The whole

thing had taken place in their absence. No European being resident in the surrounding district, the tribe was thrown on its own resources. The reason they had not taken the sick man to hospital was lack of confidence in such institutions.

"Do you mean to tell me, Father, that they *don't believe in European medicine?*"

"It's not quite like that, Monsieur——?"

"Lequeux."

"Ah! And I am Father Le Guen. No, it's not quite like that. What puts them off is—well, hospitals as such. Civil Hospitals anyway. They're so *organised* in everything they do, everything's very methodical. Sorry, this is rather difficult to explain. A Civil Hospital has a great many administrative regulations, as you know——"

"Very necessary, too."

"Just so. All this makes for a certain lack of sympathetic treatment. The atmosphere is sometimes offhand. There's a frightful amount of form-filling and red-tape. The Essazam hate that sort of thing."

"This is a very serious insinuation you're making, Father. Very serious indeed. What it amounts to is a, well, a very sharp criticism of the Public Health Service, which is doing everything it can——"

"I never doubted that for a moment, Monsieur——"

"*Lequeux.*"

"Yes, yes, I'm sorry." Le Guen was tiring of this conversation. "What I came for was to ask if a doctor possibly could be sent out to Essazam. The Chief is in a very bad way. There's no question of moving him now——"

"Of course, of course," Lequeux agreed. "We'll fix that up right away, Father. Now if you'll just follow me——"

Lequeux entered his jeep. The missionary chugged behind on his motor-bike. They pulled up before an imposing building and entered. Le Guen still trailed behind the swarthy official. The Administrator's step was brisk and smart, just like a rifleman's. In other circumstances Le Guen would have been amused. He followed Lequeux along an apparently endless corridor and finally entered a lofty, imposing office, flooded with light from a powerful electric lamp. Lequeux was already in conversation with a tall, thin young Negro; well dressed and speaking French with faint affectation.

"The Reverend Father will explain matters better than I can," Lequeux was saying.

"Where is this Reverend Father?" the Negro queried. Seeing Le Guen enter, his face lit up. "Ah, it's you!" His affability was great. "I know you, Reverend Father. I'm certain I've seen you before. When and where was it? Oh dear, it's gone: obviously a long time ago."

To Le Guen's mind this was no time for polite nothings. The missionary came straight to business.

"Monsieur, I have come to ask you for a doctor——"

"Yes, I know, I've heard all about it. I'm on duty this Sunday, so I'm coming with you myself."

"That's fine! Just fine!"

"This Chief, from all I hear, is a very good fellow. We are instructed to give him every possible attention. That is what the Chief Colonial Administrator, the Regional Administrator, that is, was just telling me——"

"*Lequeux?*"

"Of course: who else? The gentleman, who was here with you just now, has this moment gone to attend to some highly important business——"

Le Guen looked round; the Administrator had indeed vanished.

"So that's the Regional Administrator?"

"Do you mean to say you don't *know* him, Father? That is Monsieur Lequeux, Chief Colonial Administrator. Head of the Civil Service in this Territory. We're expecting him to be nominated Secretary General any day."

Clearly this fellow liked the sound of his voice. Le Guen

did not know that Pierre M—— was out for a brilliant political career. This was his reason for showing off. He was canvassing for the Legislative elections due to take place three years later.

"As I was saying," the Negro went on, "we are under instruction to look after this man—— Do please sit down! The thing is, he never deigned to ask assistance from us. Therefore I could do nothing personal, except give occasional attention to his elder son, with whom I have the honour to be acquainted. This young man leads a somewhat *irregular* life, h'm, in the city. The least one can say is that it hardly does credit to his distinguished parentage."

"Couldn't we go now?" Le Guen suggested timidly.

"Why yes, Reverend Father! Right away, right away. I'll be back in a second, Reverend Father—a second, no more——"

Off the doctor hurried. As he went out Lequeux returned, apologising for having deserted Le Guen so unceremoniously. He was even more apologetic for not having paid the Essazam tribe a visit since he took over as Regional Administrator. He was snowed under with work, he explained. Simply snowed under.

"Wait, though, Father: tomorrow—yes, *tomorrow*, no later—I'll come and say hullo to you and see how that Paramount Chief of yours is faring. His death would have very grave consequences, you know."

With that crumb of comfort he bounced out again.

Le Guen was left waiting. The promised "second or so" stretched to a quarter of an hour. The priest became thoroughly impatient. He wondered whether he were the victim of some trick.

At last the tall thin Negro returned. He burst radiantly into the office. He announced he had won a splendid victory. Managed to commandeer a Willys jeep with four-wheel transmission, instead of the usual truck, which invariably became bogged down somewhere along the mud-sodden jungle tracks.

Acidly Le Guen informed him that since Essazam was on the main eastern highway, there would be no need to go near mud-tracks. Besides, Le Guen had a motorcycle-sidecar capable of carrying at least one passenger. They could have dispensed with the Willys jeep.

On this note they set off, late in the evening. The missionary rode his motorcycle; the doctor drove his four-wheel transmission jeep. They reached Essazam a little before midnight, several hours later than Schloegel and his party. The village, which the previous day had been lethargic, was the centre of excitement. Besides the continued influx of notables from every clan in the tribe, all sorts of odd characters flocked in. Itinerant hawkers who smelt their main profit-making factor, a good crowd. Propagators of various post-war creeds, who performed a little quiet insemination and departed. Every idler and rubberneck eager for a few rousing speeches. Professional fornicators seeking "a good lay".

Shortly after midnight the doctor rejoined Le Guen. The priest was still up at the Mission. He had been awaiting his visitor. The tall Negro looked all in, but self-satisfied.

"Well, my friend?" the missionary asked. "Has he got a chance?"

The big Negro flung himself down into an armchair, sighed and shook his head.

"There's really no hope now, then?"

"Reverend Father, the Chief will be dead in a few hours."

"You will excuse me for saying this, I'm sure," Le Guen observed politely, "but everyone's been thinking the same thing for several days. Well, he isn't dead yet."

He led the doctor into the dining-room, where a meal was laid out for him. The Negro sat down to it with un-

86

concealed pleasure. Eating kept his teeth rather than his tongue engaged. Le Guen began to be better disposed towards him.

"The condition he's in," the Negro mumbled, his mouth full, chewing vigorously, "the condition he's in, he can't *not* die. Poor devil, what else is left for him? Look, another opinion might give him slightly more time to live than I have. That's only a minor detail, surely? The fact remains: this chap's done for and no mistake."

He made a striking effort to gulp down a particularly enormous mouthful.

Next morning being Monday the village was honoured in the most remarkable way. There descended upon it—not without some pomp and ceremony—a surprising number of non-African colonial officials. Among them was a distinguished Army medical officer, a colonel. He endorsed his coloured colleague's prognosis on the Chief. Lequeux himself led this distinguished visiting Commission. No sooner was he out of his jeep than he went upon a tour of inspection of the entire village. He lingered outside the Palace where groups of Elders gathered in ever-increasing numbers.

He had with him two subordinates. One was his Personal Assistant, a mulatto from the Antilles, with a fair-to-middling pedigree and a great future. The other was a very young colonial official, still sharp from a top-grade Parisian education. Looked at from a certain angle, this man's case was perplexing. His first action had been marriage. Not only had he brought his wife to Africa, but took her on all up-country bush trips. They were inseparable. To see him with his wife struck Lequeux, his official superior, as decidedly improper. Privately Lequeux was irritated. In his public capacity he considered the young couple's behaviour lacked the dignity of French officialdom. What an example to the natives! Going about with arms round each other's waists, laughing, embracing and kissing in public like a couple of moonstruck students! They gaped at everything with the uncritical admiration of tourists and asked endless questions of their mulatto friend. He took pleasure in answering at length.

Chris, who had arrived the previous evening, was keeping a discreet eye on them. He could swear that this Antilles character was "a dope who knew damn-all about anything". An opinion held by quite a few others in the village.

The presence of one Essazam boy, a skinny little creature looking far younger than his age, was still unknown to Chris. This boy had been around for a couple of days now. A ridiculous incident brought the pair together.

Chris took care to keep out of the way of the official visit. His distrust of Authority was instinctive. When the visitors departed, he settled down for a siesta on his aunt's verandah, his back resting against the wall, knees drawn up to his chin, eyes half-shut, his expression one of relaxed amiability. Suddenly a low-flying raven let fall a snake it had caught. Damaged yet not vanquished, it hit the ground near Chris, who did not even move a muscle. His coolness was legendary at college. Other villagers had been watching, with some interest, the raven's frantic attempts to control the snake; the latter's equally frantic loopings and writhings. They saw the snake fall and applauded.

One onlooker, a courageous fellow—"the Hero of Kufra", in fact—approached the snake with a long stick. He determined to finish off the raven's work—though not to the extent of eating his victim. The snake belonged to a species aggressive as it was lethal, which promised a stirring, dramatic duel.

First they circled, watching each other warily. Against this type of snake a frontal attack was out of the question. Their speed, agility and lightning striking powers are

88

fantastic. They are capable of whipping on to the stick up-raised to hit them, climbing its length like a blue streak and biting the hand that holds the stick. Since the present battlefield was enormous and bare either of bushes or undergrowth, passing this little creature's flank presented a problem. The snake was more on its guard than ever after its miraculous escape.

As the Hero of Kufra advanced, so the snake reared its small head ready to strike. If Raphael tried to outflank it, the creature flicked its entire length round in a quarter turn, preserving its position of vantage. For half an hour the Hero of Kufra tried every trick he knew. The deadlock seemed unbroken. Finally Raphael, curbing his enthusi-asm, temporarily withdrew. He mopped his sweating face, thoughtfully. Despite half-closed eyes Chris had watched every move and began to understand the stalemate. If a war threatens to become indefinite, what can one do but stop, think and invent a really decisive weapon? "You know, chum," thought Chris, studying the Hero atten-tively, "I fancy you're just beginning to think of having to use *your* atomic bomb!"

He did not suspect how right he was to prove.

In point of fact Raphael's atomic bomb was *Chris*. The Hero of Kufra suddenly turned in his direction: "Hey, you there! Why don't you come and lend a hand, instead of sitting there like a halfwit? Get yourself a stick and attack him in the rear, while I keep him occupied this side. O.K.?"

Chris did not reply. He simply sat on with half-closed eyes, as before. His only sign of having heard was a super-cilious frown, a facial gesture which, he later learnt, made him resemble a famous American film-star. He found this comparison decidedly flattering.

"What the hell? Can't you hear me?" roared Raphael. "If I hadn't come out yesterday and repaired your stinking truck, you wouldn't be sitting there like a toffee-nose

89

now! The ingratitude of it! You fancy yourself, don't you? Think you're quite something. Well, you're wrong. Want to know what you really are? I'll tell you. You're just shit, brother."

On this climax he hawked horribly and spat contempt. This achieved no reaction from Chris. The other was now nearly bursting with anger, under the cold and watchful eye of the snake. It had no intention of being off-guard during so crude a diversion.

Sitting slumped against the wall, Chris looked remote. Lots of locals were watching the Hero of Kufra, his contest no longer heroic but grotesque, attempting a two-fronted fight. Rubbernecks and no-good boyos collected. They positioned themselves behind Raphael, not anywhere near the snake.

He rattled an incredible string of insults at Chris. Bored with the whole comedy, Chris consented to speak.

"Really, what a pathetic creature you are, Raphael! It's fantastic, really it is! Where on earth did you get the idea that it takes two to finish off a poor bloody little earthworm? You know, old man, it was hardly worth your while to go off and play the big shot at Kufra, if this is all the guts you've got when you come back——"

Chris abruptly rose, took up a large lump of hardened clay he had found outside and lobbed it accurately on to the snake's tiny head. The creature thrashed its tail two or three times and expired. This done, Chris gazed at Raphael with languishing appraisal, as though the Hero of Kufra were a pretty girl. Then he said: "Oh, you poor little kid! Run home to Mummy and tell her to wash that horrible gob of yours. It *stinks*!"

A burst of jeering laughter broke from the spectators. A young boy, his mouth still wide open from his hoot of mirth, a little ashamed of his levity in this atmosphere of mourning, rushed to Chris, pumped his hand enthusiastically.

"You're unique, you really are! Always the same!"

"Hullo, it's you, is it?" Chris said. "What the hell are you doing in this ramshackle dump? Nothing but old shags here. They're falling to bits as fast as the houses."

"This is where I live, if you can imagine it. Or rather, where my father does. This is the village where he was born."

"For God's sake, what next? Anyone'd think I'd never been here before!"

After rather laborious explanations they cleared up their misunderstanding. Essazam really was the village where Bitamfombo Senior had been born. The old boy had left the district years earlier to seek his fortune in the city. He became some sort of clerk or official and never set foot in Essazam again. Thus Chris had lived for years in the village without ever seeing old Bitamfombo, or hearing his name.

For a year now his father had acquired the habit of sending young Bitamfombo on holiday to Essazam, saying it was high time the boy knew his relatives, his tribe and his part of the country. The real motive, however, was hope of reconciliation with the tribe, of patching up the quarrel his casual disappearance had produced. He wanted to retire there, having a natural nostalgia for the place.

On the other hand, his son had been born in the city, and grown up among the northern suburbs in the company of various young Arabs, whose language he now spoke. He had spent some time in a coastal town, meeting coloured children from all over Africa. He had been taught in Catholic schools when these were all there were; in Protestant ones when his father, who preferred Protestants, could afford the luxury. The old man disliked having to choose between two rival Missions. He put the boy down for a non-sectarian school whenever it could be found. Trekking around with his father, who had a weakness for strong liquor and often became a target for disciplinary measures, young Bitamfombo had slept on the floors of trucks, travelled by litter in strange primitive regions, where his father was a kind of king; even once possessed a personal bodyguard. He could speak most local dialects, knew the ritual of every religion practised in the area and was expert on the extraordinary customs of strangers and foreigners.

Meanwhile Bitama (this was the standard abbreviation of his Essazam name) took Chris off to his grandmother's house. The old lady herself was an amiable, snuffling creature. After interrogating Chris at length about his family, clan, mother's family and many such details, she declared the boys closely related upon the paternal side. Chris normally never bothered his head with such things. He knew all old people had a mania for connecting up everyone in fictitious relationships. Now, however, much to his surprise, he listened to her with rapt attenion while she breathlessly reeled off the same lists of ancestors, grandparents and forefathers with which his own mother's recitals had made him familiar.

While his grandmother chattered on, Bitama kept his eyes fixed admiringly on Chris. A beatific smile spread across his face.

"Well, what's so funny?" Chris demanded.

"Oh, nothing. I was just looking at you. My God, that old c—— of a P.T. instructor—you certainly fixed him, good and proper! He's pulled in his horns in a big way since then. Oh, you fixed him, all right."

"I had to pay a pretty stiff price for it, all the same. God knows what I had to do to keep myself from starving —and I was still keeping up my lectures all the time! I tell you, they really eat proper muck out in the suburbs. What we had as boarders was luxury by comparison. Luckily that's all over now. This year I'm living in again. I wouldn't pretend I'm not delighted. I want to get my bloody *baccalauréat* and it won't be by washing women's smalls, my God——''

"What do you think about the People's Progressive Party?" Bitama asked, his voice fairly quivering with proselytising fervour.

"What's that? Don't know it."

"Oh come off it! I can't believe you! Why lie to me, of all people? I know you: you're a cautious, secretive sort of chap. But you can trust me. Look, the first thing I'm going to do this term is to take out a Party card. Come on, talk to me about the P.P.P."

"I don't get you, boy. I tell you, I haven't a clue what the P.P.P. is. If that weren't true, I wouldn't say so. Why the hell should I lie to you? It's crazy."

Bitama hesitated, staring at Chris suspiciously. Chris was the frankest of men by nature. The obvious sincerity of his disclaimers finally convinced Bitama, who took on rather a disappointed air.

"From the way you behave," he said, "anyone would assume you were a member of the P.P.P."

"Why? Have militant P.P.P. members some special code of behaviour?"

"Yes, indeed they have."

"Like the Boy Scouts?"

"Ah, no, *not* like the Boy Scouts! Nothing artificial. If they conduct themselves in a particular way, it's not carrying out rules. It's just that that's the way they are; nothing else to it."

Since his old grandmother kept interrupting to impart some fresh genealogical detail, Bitama, whose patience was fraying, suggested he and Chris might talk elsewhere. They went to Chris's aunt's house, empty since the Chief's wife and her companions lived on the sick man's doorstep. Bitama had cigarettes with him. Chris broke one of his rules by accepting and smoking several. He remarked that anyone as poor as he was ought to keep down expenses.

93

Bitama seemed in a state of nervous tension and excitement. He launched himself into queerly bookish arguments about this and that. He appeared ill at ease. He did not seem well. His extreme scrawniness made him appear thirteen when he was at least four years older.

Suddenly he blurted out: "I'm absolutely staggered by your indifference to the P.P.P., Chris. How can it be possible that the cleverest, best educated people among the younger generation—the *élite*, in fact—are so lukewarm where the P.P.P. is concerned? I just don't understand it. Haven't you come across this bizarre state of affairs yourself? Well, I suppose 'bizarre' is one way of putting it. Look: here we are on this f——ing planet and we're Blacks. It's no good looking around for great Black leaders, here, in books, or anywhere else. You can examine the portraits of as many famous men as you like, you won't find anyone looking like us. So you begin to feel lonely. You'd like to *invent* such men, whose skins are as black as yours—men you could see all around you, *real* men, men who exist. You'd turn yourself into God, just to do that. Haven't you ever felt that way yourself?"

Chris reflected. He was inwardly surprised at Bitama's sudden volubility. In college he was a quiet, uncommunicative sort of person. This was true of term-time. During holidays the prospect of several weeks' liberty went, quite literally, to his adolescent head. He was like a dog off the lead. In the end Chris said they had too much difficult work to do in class to have time for that sort of thing. Bitama snorted with laughter. Then he flushed up and said: "For the first time in our country's history we've got a party that's offering us a platform for *our own* great men. That's why I go for the P.P.P., Chris. It's only natural, isn't it? Suppose you were watching your brother competing in a cross-country marathon—wouldn't you feel miserable if he came trailing in last?"

"Certainly not. I should say to him, Look, chum, you

just aren't cut out to be a long-distance runner. Go and see if Mama hasn't got a nice meaty tit-bit stowed away somewhere. Have a good tuck-in on me. That's what I'd say. Just as there are individuals who are simply incapable of getting anywhere, so the same happens with certain races. Both have to make the best of a bad job. They aren't like the rest. They're lacking in vitality or something. That's all there is to it. I've someone like that in the family, my elder brother. He can't do anything bar make a bloody fool of himself. He just hasn't what it takes. If you really want to know, I feel like the spectator of some terrible tidal wave that's washing everything away. My kind of spectator will try to save one possession from destruction, and one only. That which is closest to his heart."

At first this outburst of Chris's scandalised Bitama. Despite himself he was struck by the extreme individualism of the final part of the speech. Nothing if not partisan, he promised to think about what Chris had said.

Chris rose and walked across to a big cask, the top of which was covered with an even bigger banana-leaf. As he bent over the cask, he thought Bitama a lazy sort of ass. He would have better things to consider were he obliged to provide his own clothes, school-books and pocket-money. Not to mention buying knick-knacks for a small sister. Having said so, he put one ear to the side of the cask. A faint bubbling sound reached him. An expression of intense pleasure lit up his face. When Bitama enquired what the cask contained, Chris told him it was the raw material for—well—a work of art. His aunt had prepared it. She had not taken the appropriate action when her distinguished husband fell ill. If Chris had not turned up, heaven knew what might have happened!

"Dear God, think of all that lovely stuff going to waste! Cassava, bananas, ripe maize—best quality material, every ounce of it. The first two bottles will be at least seventy-five per cent proof."

"Good God," Bitama said, eyes widening. He had understood at last. "Do you mean to say you're *distilling alcohol?*"

"Well, why shouldn't I?"

With that they plunged into argument about drunkenness. Bitama claimed that Chris, by distilling strong liquor, was playing straight into the hands of the colonialists. Chris roared with laughter at this. He said he couldn't care less about the colonialists: all that interested him was making a little spot cash for Grigri and himself.

"Look, Bitama, you get dough from your father, right? Well, then, I suppose you wouldn't shell out a bit of it for me?"

"We haven't got all that much money," Bitama said hastily. "I mean, Dad drinks a hell of a lot, and—and—well, he's got three wives and ten kids: it does mount up rather."

Chris whistled. "What a family! There's three of us, with one girl and a half-wit Mum on the side. Come on; I've got to get cracking right away. Look, you know so bloody much about everything—tell me, what do you make of our beloved Pharaoh at the moment?"

"It appears," said Bitama, his voice sceptical yet questioning, "that he's been converted to Catholicism."

"Conversion's a strong word in the circumstances. My aunt told me what really happened. They caught him at a moment when he was no longer capable of telling them what his opinions actually were."

Bitama gave a sharp laugh. "Nowadays Catholicism is nothing but a kind of baited nigger-trap."

They began discussing the various elders. Bitama spoke endlessly in their praise, lauding their wisdom, courage and traditional skills, not to mention their tribal solidarity —all characteristically Negro qualities, it appeared.

"It's not hard to see that *you* grew up in the city," Chris remarked chaffingly. "Do you really think all that

96

much of the old shags? You're a bit like Mama in some ways——"

"Oh yes? Halfwitted, am I?"

"No, old chap. You know I didn't mean that. What I'm after is this. Mama says one moment that we've to honour and venerate our eldest brother. This is what our ancestors have always done. It worked very well for them. An instant later she's talking about the Chief. Refers to him as a polygamous old swine. As though polygamy weren't just as much a legacy from our ancestors! Can you honestly say there's any consistency of thought in that kind of thing? Well, you're much the same yourself. You call yourself a revolutionary. At the same time you're lost in admiration for those crapulous old dotards representing the most shameful, disgusting elements surviving from our history. Always supposing we *had* a history. I don't know, myself. Anyway, I don't give a damn."

"You despise them, don't you?"

"Who, the old shags? No! I've never despised anyone in my life. That doesn't stop me thinking sometimes they're lazy, greedy, senile morons, nattering away aimlessly. They make a miserable mess of anything they attempt. Take all these elders who've rolled up lately. What are they here *for*? The Chief's ill. All right—and then what? Must the whole world stand still just because of that? F——ing nonsense! If I were in their shoes, I'd be out at work—as I am now, in fact. You're all right: you've an old man in the Administration, you lucky sod."

"I never thought you were like this," Bitama said earnestly. "Do you know how I'd describe your outlook? Grossly materialistic."

"There you go with your long words again! Listen, tell me, do you reckon your father'd cough up—at least for the basic minimum? Ah Christ, when you spend all your time with your nose stuck in some highbrow book I suppose you reckon *words* are good enough currency——

97

All right, we won't bring *that* subject up again. You can stay there if you like, you won't be in my way. Well—are you going to help me?"

. . . It all happened in the most extraordinary way, Mama, and I should need reams of paper and a month's leisure to give you every complex twist and turn in the game. When I returned from Ongola, your Bantu king was practically at death's door. As I write these words we are all waiting; resigned to the worst. Any moment now, there can be little doubt, his spirit will return to its Creator. . . .

Then, in a flash, the Reverend Father Le Guen, Superior of the Catholic Mission in Essazam, was caught up in a world which seemed compounded of horror and savagery. Howls and shrieks burst upon his ears so that he was shaken, despite himself. The air felt unpleasantly heavy, as though some sinister electric charge had been passed through it. The darkness terrified him most. Macabre, impenetrable, spine-chilling blackness of the night. To discover what had happened meant going out into that darkness.

. . . That's it, Mama! Yes: it's all over now. It happened just as I was writing the word 'Creator': by such a thread do men's lives hang. Our beloved Bantu king is no more. How can I describe what is happening here, dearest Mama? He is no——

Unearthly silence had fallen. It spread and lurked in every shadowy corner; its touch chilled the air. "He isn't dead after all," thought Le Guen, knowing his flock and their customs so well. The Chief must have just fainted. "Dear God, I can't stand any more of this!"

He found Brother Joseph, who quite clearly was in an equal state of agitation.

"All these fancy goings-on keep me from my beauty sleep," Schloegel told him peevishly.

Le Guen sighed. "Me too."

"He's funking the issue in proper style, isn't he? Why can't he hurry up and decide one way or the other?"

"I was asking myself the same question."

"You know," said the boy Gustave, appearing unobserved beside them, "you know, when a sick man passes a certain point, he doesn't die after all. That's what they're saying in the village. It's so long since the Chief *ought* to have died that they reckon he won't."

"Oh Lord," said Brother Joseph, "for heaven's sake don't *you* start again, you little horror!"

"But it's true," the boy insisted. "No one in the village thinks he's going to die any more."

Le Guen burst out laughing. It struck him that a row between Brother Joseph and Gustave would be the most unlikely outcome of the affair—indeed, the Chief's most remarkable achievement since his illness.

The boy continued, half triumphantly: "In fact, Father, your troubles are only just beginning."

"How do you make that out?" Le Guen demanded aggressively.

"You've given the Chief Extreme Unction. That means you accepted Yosifa's baptism as valid."

"Well?" asked Le Guen, already with a shrewd notion what Gustave meant.

"Let's say the Chief recovers. He's a man who's been baptised—a Christian. So he'll have to give up his wives, won't he? Can you see *that* happening in a hurry?"

The two missionaries stood stock-still. Something was going wrong with this boy. He asked far too many awkward questions.

Le Guen had never suspected the extent of Gustave's genuine anxiety. When he had met them on the road, Le Guen naturally assumed the boy was inspired by Providence, God or whatever entity a priest might legitimately attribute his good fortune to. He began to wonder instead what devil lurked in this snotty lad's skull. Le Guen found himself beginning to *desire* the Chief's death, as though to win some bet with Gustave. "And that," he told himself in alarm, "is where a lifetime of spreading the Gospel can get you!"

The following day he forced himself to confess all this, in a letter to his mother. The composition gave him considerable trouble.

Less than a week later the Chief was on his feet again.

It had not been his original intention to arise. He only wanted to see whether he still could control his limbs. The attempt proved successful. To his own astonishment and that of his wives, who, after their long bout of nursing duty, were distinctly drowsy, he actually walked out of Makrita's house, wobbling a bit on his shrunken legs. Taking no notice of the hot wind whipping round him and rustling the palm-trees that lined the square, he instinctively went in the general direction of his Palace.

He tottered through the village, happy as a child rediscovering the outside world. He advanced with a slightly drunken gait. He was intoxicated by the fading darkness, the glowing dawn and the wind breathing fresh life into him.

He reached the Palace and mounted the steps like a somnambulist. With some effort he reached the upper floor. He went on to the balcony, resting his arms on the balustrade. It felt unfamiliar. He decided it should come alive under him, like an affectionate wife, to put him at ease. He stood watching the elements.

First, the clouds scudded wildly across the sky. Thunder rolled and grumbled. The sky became a lurid glow, streaked with blood red.

Suddenly he heard the quick drumming of rain. Quickly it swept across the village in a torrential onslaught. To him it resembled a horde, surging over Essazam, trampling and devastating it. How quickly they passed. Soon they were far away, the storm carrying them. A million tree-tops shivered, tossing and trembling. On his left, towards the East, a huge oily stain spread across the sky, gradually lightening to yellow as it expanded.

During his convalescence the Chief remained in bed, dozing, receiving his counsellors, elders, wives, children, and anyone else to whom he was obliged to be reasonably polite. Reverend Father Le Guen was a frequent visitor. He arrived in the mornings, often at about ten o'clock. He spent little time in the antechamber. Directly he appeared there was action. Everyone babbled apologies for keeping him waiting and he was shown straight in. He was in an excellent position to observe, at leisure, how quickly his new convert was reverting to type as his health improved. Gustave's words on that fateful night remained to him a source of alarm and despondency. How could one ever make a real Christian out of this savage, when he did not know abstinence or self-discipline?

When he discussed the Chief's baptism with him, his tone veered between the playful and the pathetic. He talked about his convert's new family, the Church Universal, dwelling upon the fact that, because of his illness, the Chief had been fortunate enough to receive baptism at the hand of his mother (or aunt). He besought the Chief to adopt a way of life in keeping with his baptism. Le Guen threatened Divine Wrath, fanning the flames of eternal hell-fire under his nose, forewarning him against the countless ways in which the Devil was liable to tempt into sin a soul aspiring towards God.

Le Guen proselytised with zealous enthusiasm, but the Chief was largely impervious to such exhortations. He often brushed them aside irritably. He did not appear to be renouncing any worldly joys. Instead, he regaled his old friend with his experiences on "the Other Side". He recalled in detail a meeting with his ancestors and the souls of former members of the tribe. The deceased had assembled in a vast gathering for the occasion under the aegis of Akomo himself.

After a long palaver they had addressed the Chief roughly in these words: "What are *you* doing here, when the tribe of the living has not dispensed with your services? You are a true son of Akomo. It would have given us indescribable pleasure to have welcomed you finally amongst us. Still we on the Other Side can afford to be patient. But what about the living? Could they do without you? No! You must go back among them; find your way to their world once more. When the time comes, we will summon you ourselves."

Akomo himself had taken the Chief aside and offered private consolation. In the eyes of the dead the sacrifice demanded was considerable. They bade him return to the world, a world full of unforeseeable hazards, many inexplicable, if not senseless.

"It was a long journey back," he would say, finally, yawning. This was how he concluded this story every time.

Yosifa also called at the Palace with touching regularity. She showed a praiseworthy desire to keep her resuscitated son free from sin. She brought great powers of persuasion. She was steeped in all the superstitious beliefs of the tribe, and for all her disclaimers, shared many herself. In quick succession she produced dark hints, subtle threats, lengthy argument, bursts of hysteria, dumb misery, great sighs and extravagant displays of pathos. Each mood had a matching style of speech. Her rhetorical talent was as varied as it was sustained. All this left its mark upon the poor Chief, only just free of the dreams and fantasies of delirium. Above all, she was his aunt. In Essazam parlance, his mother. At this period there survived among older members of the tribe a specialised fetichism. This could embrace not only the mother herself but any person who, however imperfectly, symbolised the myth of maternal functions.

Yosifa, then, finally shocked her 'son' into decision. She did so by means of a dream, which could have been fictional or genuine. In it she was visited by ancestral ghosts of ancestors, who bade her go to the Chief at daybreak and say to him: "My beloved son, last night I saw in a dream the departed spirits of So-and-So and Such-and-Such. They told me to pass on this message to you. Accept the consequences of baptism. Send your wives back to their clans, keeping only the one who is to be your spouse in the eyes of God and to whom you will be joined in wedlock, according to the rites of Le Guen's faith. God let you return to the world of the living, so that you might begin a new life as a Christian. If you wish, after death, to receive the position due to your noble blood, you must agree, once and for all, to become a Christian. That is the message which our ancestors send you, with the approval of Akomo himself."

Yosifa punctuated the message with sobs, sniffs, lamentations, rolling of the eyeballs and similar dramatic tricks. All had proved persuasive during the course of her long life. The same day she was succeeded at the convalescent's bedside by the Negro doctor. He remonstrated severely with his patient over the excesses in which the latter was already beginning to indulge. The combined pressure and influences had effect. Hardly had the doctor left than the Chief summoned his young brother.

"No one is to leave for home yet," the Chief told him. "All the distinguished visitors from the various Essazam clans here in this village must remain here for the time being. I want them to take part in the feast to celebrate my recovery. At the end there are several important decisions I shall have to announce."

The news spread rapidly. Essazam prepared itself for the festivities. Those two old rogues, Ondoua and Ndibidi, went tirelessly from house to house, vying with one another in eloquence and voracity. The story-tellers and ballad-mongers (who contrived to enhance tawdry imaginations with fine leopard-skin costumes, in which they whirled round like dervishes) now hinted at their craft. Eager listeners were given peeps into Akomo's fantastic kingdom, with its concubines and warriors. Women burst into lyric song, improvising delightful verses celebrating the joys of love. Palm-wine flowed in rivers; chickens, sheep and goats were sacrificed by the hundred. From late evening till dawn the priests' sacrificial cudgels cracked down on their victims' skulls. Day and night the young folk fornicated tirelessly. The only person to keep cool in the midst of general hysteria was Chris. He made money out of it, hand over fist.

On the fourth day of these celebrations the doctor visited Le Guen at the Mission and they had a long discussion.

"Father," he said, "I have taken the liberty of calling upon you to suggest that this Chief of yours should take rather better care of his health."

"Oh?" Le Guen spoke with acidity. "Why should you bother? Why do you want him to take care of himself? Look, my friend: you know perfectly well that nothing will happen to him. A few days ago, if you remember, you were convinced he'd be dead in four to six hours. So was I. I had some excuse for thinking so. Well, my friend, he isn't dead. Put yourself in his position. When a man recovers from *that* sort of illness, why should he watch his health?"

"All the same, he's going it a bit strong," the doctor insisted. "Heavens, Father, you ought to see him! Drinking and gorging. The man's an absolute pig! One of these days he'll succumb to a really bad attack of indigestion and this time he won't recover."

"Don't play the prophet with me, my friend," Le Guen said, despondently.

"Father, whatever you think, please keep an eye on him. Try to, anyway. Lequeux wants him to stay alive, you know. He says the old boy's death would give everyone a real headache. For instance, as things are at the moment, we'd have a difficult time arranging for his successor. All his male children are still very young—apart from Maurice, of course, but he's a proper no-good boyo. Have you heard about Maurice's latest exploit, Father? I bet you'd never guess——"

"Come on, tell me."

"Breaking and entering, no less. Luckily it was a shop belonging to some Greek or other and he got off with a few months inside. Suppose he'd exercised his talents at the expense of a French businessman, Father? What then? He'd have been a cert for ten years' forced labour. My God, these young idiots!"

"Does his father know what's happened?"

"No. I've taken great care that he doesn't hear a thing about it. What would be the point of worrying him? Why bother the tribe? That was also Lequeux's opinion, I may add. I'm sure you understand."

"Might one enquire, my friend, just why you are showing such peculiar solicitude on Maurice's account?"

The doctor gave an embarrassed grin. He had decided that Le Guen was a missionary with whom it was risky, if not positively dangerous, to be confidential. He determined to reveal one of the motives impelling him to cultivate Maurice's friendship. His choice fell upon the more harmless, less exotic reason. He took advantage of the opening to give a detailed exposition of his ideas on democracy. They boiled down to a thousand and one foolproof ways of getting himself elected to office.

Here he gave the fat, self-satisfied laugh of a man about to play an abominable trick upon his best friend. To Le Guen's question he replied that, hailing originally from the coast, he had a greater instinct for diplomacy than cloddish peasants from the interior. He was not afraid of any local candidates in the 1951 elections. He was sure to defeat them. He went so far as to hint at some arrangement with Le Guen. The priest had the ear of many influential members of the Essazam tribe. The doctor considered he might prove a more useful supporter than Maurice, whose credit grew daily shakier. Le Guen promised to note these enthusiastic suggestions. The doctor imagined the whole thing to be "in the bag"; a highly erroneous assumption.

When he had gone, Le Guen found himself reflecting that this young doctor was rather a likable rogue.

The same day the Reverend Father mustered all his determination and will-power and sought audience with the Chief. What took place no one discovered. Directly Le Guen left, the Chief summoned his brother, telling him to send away all the Palace wives.

"Except the one and only wife to whom I shall be married in the eyes of God."

"And which one might that be?" Mekanda enquired cautiously.

The Chief sniggered. "Which one? Ah-ha. *She* knows and *I* know." And that was that.

The news that the Chief was repudiating all his wives, save one single lady whom he would wed before God and live with for the rest of his life, as Le Guen's faith enjoined, exploded amid the festivities. Everyone rushed to question Mekanda. He found himself hemmed in by a vast mob, convinced that he knew divine secrets. His course was to take refuge in cheerful, quite genuine ignorance. He had no exact knowledge, he declared. "Is the Chief *really* putting away his wives?" they insisted.

"Well, yes." Such was his definite information.

"On what date would the Church wedding take place?" Mekanda protested that had he been told he would have announced it publicly. Well, then, who *was* the one and only wife the Chief was going to marry before God? Mekanda said he had been informed that only the lady herself knew. . . .

The confusion assumed vast proportions. To avoid revealing his intentions in detail the Chief refused to receive visitors apart from Mekanda and Le Guen. In this chaotic situation the Chief's eldest son, Maurice, made his mark. No one in Essazam realised that Maurice was a pimp and an old lag. Had the facts been public knowledge the tribe would not have bothered overmuch. They remained indifferent to what better-informed folk might consider disgraceful. But what Maurice said, and his obvious conviction, produced a sensation. He was a dramatic forewarning of conflict to come. The village was the theatre where this conflict would be resolved. In exhausted irritation this heir-presumptive made the following statement. The people who asked who the one lucky wife was to be surely insulted his mother, Makrita. No one could suppose that this one lucky wife was any other than Makrita.

The Christian community in Essazam was suspicious about this detail in the story. They made up for their lack of numbers by zealous promoting of the conversion. They held meetings to celebrate the Chief's enrolment, extolling Le Guen's miraculous achievement in snatching him back from death. They made up epic poems on the subject and wove impromptu ballads round it. They even conducted triumphal processions through the streets. In their midst rode a man wearing a long white robe—recalling the entry of Christ into Jerusalem.

Makrita could talk of nothing but the magnificent ceremony to mark the Chief's entry into the Church; the long train of worshippers who would attend; the feast she would provide for members of his clan. Makrita's boastfulness apart, the Chief's other wives maintained a hopeful silence. Each was mentally totting up her moments of intimacy with the old pasha; the degree of pleasure which he apparently obtained. Women had this odd delusion that nothing matched the special quality of the pleasure *they* gave a man. They were often convinced that having had them once, he would be unable to do without them. It was a simple matter for each genuinely to believe that *she* was the lucky one he would marry in the eyes of God.

Days passed. The clan elders, being unable to bear the suspense of waiting, sent Mekanda as their delegate to the Chief, exhorting him to give them a clear-cut decision. The Chief had a natural aversion to taking any final step. On the other hand he was aware of having shilly-shallied too long. He made up his mind to clinch the matter.

"Oh, go and tell them how things stand," he said to his brother. "You know my decision. Tell them."

From this instant things began to move with a vengeance.

"As our forefathers used to say," Ndibidi observed, "Woman is an ear of maize. Any man with good teeth can have a nibble at her." With this remark he picked out a large hunk of mutton, measuring it up with thumb and forefinger. The thicker the meat, the better he liked it. Gripping it firmly in both enormous paws, he began eating.

Ondoua gave the smile of a fencer who has just scored a point through his opponent's clumsiness.

"They were right," he said. "They had another proverb, too. 'Woman is a slender palm-tree and any man with a good belt can get up her.'"

Not to be outdone, he grabbed the remaining piece of meat—somewhat hastily, though it was clearly his by right, since only the two of them were eating out of this particular dish. The others present watched the little scene closely: Mekanda with some disgust, Makrita and her children with fleeting smiles. The Chief's brother considered these smiles indicative of guile. They alerted him.

He cleared his throat. "I'd very much like to know why you asked me here, Makrita."

Ndibidi interrupted. "Come over and eat with us, boy!" He had some difficulty in enunciation since his mouth was crammed full. In speaking he emitted a shower of crumbs and other scraps. Ondoua seconded his invitation, equally at choking-point.

Mekanda declined and said he was not hungry. Actually he could not bear rooting in the same trough as the two old pigs.

"No. I'm not hungry. There's only one thing I want. To know the reason for my invitation. If there's nothing behind it, I'm off."

He did not miss the quick hint of appeal Makrita gave her son. The young man sat opposite her, his back against the wall. His hat pulled over one eye, he chewed at a straw. In response to this appeal, and also to precipitate a previously arranged scene, Maurice arose. He lounged slowly across to his uncle, frowning fiercely, his visible eye narrowed threateningly. He looked for all the world like a third-rate ham actor. A few inches away from Mekanda he stopped and said, in attempted suavity: "Tell me, my friend, would you dare repeat here what you have been broadcasting round the village? I am informed that you claim my father intends to put aside all his wives, including my mother. Will you repeat this dastardly suggestion in the presence of these two worthy gentlemen?"

Mekanda answered: "Since when have they become worthy gentlemen?" He thought this remark likely to annoy his nephew enough to bring him to the point.

"I have always regarded them as highly respectable

109

citizens," Maurice said, his voice angry. "What are you insinuating?"

"Heigh-ho! Man is a changeable creature."

"Leave your uncle alone, Maurice!" the two old men begged. "Please, won't you come and sit down?"

Makrita joined in the chorus, suddenly scared, for the argument was taking on an ugly tone. One unfortunate word, one misinterpreted glance, would be enough to bring the two men to blows.

Makrita originally had done her best to create this situation. Frantic by reason of her rejection as wife *par excellence*, at her wits' end to regain her husband, she was a prey to idiotic impulses. She had thought to intimidate Mekanda. He alone had access to the Chief during convalescence and possibly exerted some influence. She was convinced of her own unique rights over the Chief's person. Her belief was more unshakable than ever. She could overlook the fact that he had married fresh young wives and taken them into the bed from which she had been ejected. To *repudiate* her was going too far. Such was her present state of mind. Le Guen's teaching and catechism had helped to bring her to the edge of exasperation.

No one was more delighted by her husband's conversion. "Why," she asked herself, "could not she have taken him by the hand and led him, like a child, to Christ's feet?" She had preceded him in the Faith. She had made his path easier. It would have been simple.

Accordingly she had launched her explosion. At any moment things might get out of hand.

"This is a trap," Mekanda declared repeatedly. He ignored the two old men's protests.

"My dear Maurice," Mekanda went on. "Why should I not accede to your request? It is true the Chief told me to make a public announcement saying he was putting aside all his wives, except one——"

"But *which one?*" Maurice hissed, doing his best to

keep calm, but inwardly anxious. He was terrified by his present position. He could hardly retreat without losing face. He was desperate for the whole thing to finish, being a pathetic creature, full of self-pity.

"Which one?" Mekanda repeated. "Which one? Anaba, obviously."

"It's a lie!" Maurice screamed, leaping up. This movement sent him backwards instead of forwards. He ended back against the wall. He gave the impression of being about to spring. Considering his neat withdrawal, this was rather clever.

"It's a lie! Papa could never have said such a thing! Did you put the idea into his head? Oh, I know you! How you adore a bit of intrigue. It sticks out a mile what it is you're after. You've worked it all out, haven't you? You reckon the Chief can't last long after this illness. When he dies, you'll marry Anaba. His other wives will have been repudiated; their children disinherited. So, you reckon to be sitting pretty as the next Chief. Don't try and pretend you aren't doing your damnedest to discredit me in the eyes of the whole tribe. You're sweating blood trying to convince the elders that I'm unfit to succeed my father. You might as well give up, my friend. You can't stop my being the legitimate heir. Do you hear me? *I'm the heir!*"

Standing before his nephew, taking stock as he ranted on, Mekanda felt surprised rather than angry. He wondered how far Makrita would go. The recriminations of Maurice had doubtless originated from his mother. He laughed, yawned, affected not to have understood a word of his nephew's spluttering diatribe. This was a cruelly ironic drawing of attention to Maurice's slight stammer. He went so far as to suggest that his nephew was drunk.

Screaming that he had been insulted, Maurice sprang forward as though to attack his uncle. Being rather a coward and less angry than he pretended, he was careful to put the brakes on, so to speak, before the two old men and his mother came in front of his target. He did it so cleverly that anyone who was not a close watcher or who heard about the incident at second-hand, would suppose that Maurice was prevented from beating up his uncle by the strenuous intervention of a third party.

It looked as though trouble were in the offing. The two old men averted it by appealing to Mekanda, as being the elder and therefore more reasonable of the two, to break off the argument like a gentleman and leave the house. Maurice's sister, the tart, sat on one side watching the proceedings with that half-somnolent expression often found among very stupid women—or animals whose behaviour is conditioned by elementary stimuli. This was distressing in the extreme and bound to give a bad impression of the tribe as a whole, represented here by members of all three generations.

Mekanda stood his ground, determined to hear his nephew out. Maurice accused his uncle point-blank of sleeping with Anaba; of begetting the child she was now bearing. He challenged Mekanda to deny this relationship with the girl.

Maurice remained leaning against the wall, his mother in front of him now, her body protecting his. (Not that it was much of a body! Its dimensions had but a distant resemblance to the normal female figure.) Despite tearful prayers and supplications by the two dotards, Mekanda demanded that if Maurice were a man at all, he should repeat his crazy accusations. Makrita put both hands over his mouth to stop him. The wretched youth, reacting just like any spoilt child, made it a point of honour to roar out these scandalous accusations again. After all, it was his mother who had put them into his head.

Grimly determined, Mekanda tried to get his hands on Maurice. The way always was barred by the Aged Twins, pot-bellied, over-full, grimacing and belching madly. Cecilia's cow-like gaze, stupefied by continual fornication, became more somnolent than ever. While struggling with the two old men, Mekanda yelled out that Maurice could not have invented these filthy allegations. He lived in the city and had no knowledge of events in Essazam. The city seemed to be treating him well, too, Mekanda added ironically.

This was a common remark in Essazam and up-country; usually it was applied to any young man who lived in town without seeming to have a regular job. Quite wrongly Maurice assumed it to be alluding to his recent bother with Authority. He flung off his mother's restraining hand and hurled himself at his uncle. With one gigantic effort Mekanda succeeded in shaking loose the encumbering old men. Neither combatant had any idea of dodging or weaving. They met in a head-on collision. Despite this, they seemed untroubled by the shock of impact. If they recoiled a little, it was merely to work up speed for a second go. Next moment they again came at one another full tilt, heads down, necks hunched, shoulders forward, like two rams in the rutting season, fighting for their favourite hind. There was no science about this fight, much less style. Both lacked elementary notions of self-protection.

After a few of these head-on collisions Maurice seemed somewhat shaken and changed tactics. He aimed a terrific kick at his uncle's shins. Mekanda, whirling his clenched right fist aloft like some primitive club, gave the ex-jailbird a frightful pummelling. Maurice lost his footing and stumbled over one of the rattan chairs, which had been in his way before. He scrambled clear and, scared of Mekanda catching him off his guard again, shot into the courtyard. Here he awaited his uncle, to all appearances as firm on his feet as ever. Mekanda followed him out and immediately tussled with him again. Vaguely recalling some lessons in unarmed combat, Maurice managed to pin both his uncle's arms by squeezing them against his own ribs and made a valiant effort to throw him. All that happened, however, was that both fighters spun round like huge entangled tops, until Mekanda, stronger and cooler-headed, tripped his nephew and stretched him on his back in the dust. Then he set to methodically, aiming blows with deliberation, even raising his victim's head to get a better swipe at his jaw. Poor Maurice went through a frightful time. His tongue lolled out of the corner of his mouth. Cecilia put the finishing touches to the exhibition by taking a machete to Mekanda. She gave him two gigantic cuts across the shoulderblades, laying the flesh wide open, and would have gone on until she killed him if it had not been for Chris. Abandoning his golden rule of remaining a spectator, he came over, jammed one knee in the small of the would-be murderess's back and bent her arm until she was compelled to drop her weapon.

People came running from all sides. Mekanda was carried off, smothered in blood. Maurice was lifted groggily to his feet. Cecilia and her mother were nearly lynched by the crowd. Cursing and swinging his fists, Chris did his best to protect them—more for the sport of it than belief in their cause. Everyone asked how on earth it could have happened. When they learnt that the tribe's two most venerable patriarchs had actually witnessed the affair, they looked for them to hear their version. The old men were nowhere to be found. The crowd cursed them heartily, saying that the tribe must be crazy to rely on them for anything. A moment later they completely forgot about the shortcomings of these ancient greybeards and were engaged upon their daily business.

The only noteworthy consequence was that the Chief emerged from his Palace, appearing in the village square for everyone to see. He slowly advanced—perhaps 'glided' would be the better term—moving like a ghost dressed in blue cotton trousers and khaki shirt with decorative epaulettes. His feet were naked and big as ever. His expression was somewhat strained and haggard, partly from anger, partly from shortness of breath. Though he had not lost all that much weight, he looked taller than ever. Some people deliberately walked past him for a closer glimpse. A few Doubting Thomases contrived to touch him and shake his hand. As he passed by each little group they whispered about him behind his back, showing a kind of unwilling admiration for a man who could come back from the dead and yet remain the same person.

He walked to the threshold of a certain hut. Outside stood a tall, thinnish young man—Chris. Observing what appeared to be a sleepwalker making straight for him, he stood politely aside to let the Chief enter. He did not go immediately into the house. He stopped, eyeing the young man searchingly. Inside he found a woman who had once been his wife. He addressed her in very general terms.

"I told you to get out days ago. What in hell are you waiting for? Do you want me to go back upon my decision? Because if so, you're wasting your time."

The Chief left the hut, again pausing for a moment opposite Chris. As before, Chris met his eye and stared him out—a little arrogantly perhaps, but without rancour. Yet he was on the brink of tears, thinking of his aunt's recent humiliation. Without appearing to pay any attention he had heard every word of the Chief's diatribe. His glance followed him as the old rogue barged his way into the next-door hut, where he proceeded to humiliate another woman who had been his wife for many years.

Chris returned to his aunt, sitting on the bed beside her. Big tears rolled gently down her cheeks.

"She should not cry," he thought. "She ought to stop herself. Why do people always let themselves be trampled upon in this way? She ought to stop herself, even if she has to grit her teeth. What's the use of parading her un-happiness?"

His aunt's submissive attitude repelled him. She was too sensitive and subservient. He owed much to this woman. She had given him what little tenderness his hazardous childhood had known. His own mother had not spoilt him; she had to divide her attention among numerous children and never pretended to love them equally.

All he could say in consolation was: "Come on, let's go. If you stay with us you won't feel you're on your own. Your sister's a bit hard to get on with, but I've managed pretty well so far."

He was trying desperately to imagine his aunt's misery. In the end life had given her nothing; not even a child. Yet there was nothing more he could say to her.

Without looking at him, she whispered: "You've got the chance to be a fine man, Chris."

"I know," he said, sincerely.

His aunt corrected him. "No, you don't altogether. If, one day, you have children—and that's something I desire with all my heart—make sure they're all boys, Chris. I know you: if you had a daughter, you'd certainly end up killing some man just because he'd made your little girl suffer. You see, since you're a man, you don't know how we women are specially made for suffering. How long has it been all told? Fifteen years I've been here, perhaps more. Living in a village I thought my own, and in a house I supposed to belong to me; looking after a man I imagined to be my husband. Yet in a moment he can come striding in and say to me: 'Get out of here, I don't want you any more—you mean nothing to me, you don't belong here.' That, after those terrible weeks we've just lived through because of his illness! If I'd suspected that the whole thing just wasn't worth the trouble. That I was wasting my life! If only I'd suspected——"

"Oh, come now! You haven't wasted your time——"

"Haven't I? What good has it all been, Chris? I wish you'd tell me. Why have I worked, slaved and suffered so long? Who will give me a plot to dig or a house to live in."

"But I said you were to come and live with us——"

"Poor Chris! You're still very young, aren't you? Listen, darling. A woman without a husband is nothing. I couldn't marry again; I'm too old."

"You'll come and live with us," Chris insisted. "You'll be absolutely free. You can work in your own fields. Go to market at Vimili and sell your produce, just as Mama does, and spend your money as you please. There now!"

"Spend my money as I please? What use would that be to me? You just can't understand, Chris, it's no good."

Chris helped her to pack up her few belongings; they did not weigh much. They went into two cases: a big one which Chris carried; another, much smaller, of which his aunt took charge herself.

That same day the Chief made further dispositions concerning his children by his repudiated wives. Most of these were still very young; Maurice and Cecilia were exceptions. They found themselves handed over to various highly respectable housewives around the village, who were to feed them and bring them up. He reassured these fostermothers in person, telling them that he would take care of things himself. They need have no fear on the grounds of expenditure.

Before his illness the Chief had been a cheerful, happy-go-lucky sort of person; his present firmness—harshness, even—caused consternation. The Essazam tribe, an indolent lot detesting over-haste, suspicious even of ordinary hurry, were amazed by the revolutionary measures this conversion had caused. No one had guessed its consequences would include stern authority by the Chief.

Chris was in a hurry to quit the village. Despite the lateness of the hour he had set out with his aunt. Such

was the state of public feeling that he was soon inter-
cepted by a crowd of people, shouting the odds. They
condemned his hurried departure as conduct befitting
a townsman. They went so far as to suggest that the Chief's
orders were not to be taken literally. For the time being,
therefore, the pair returned to the home of Chris's aunt.

The many wise men of the tribe consulted together.
Agreement was unanimous. Even Yosifa, surprisingly
enough, concurred. The situation lacked immediate
urgency. Hasty, ill-considered action would be regrettable.
They were of the opinion that the Chief's ex-wives (who
in any case remained the brides of the Ebazok clan as a
whole) should for the present continue to reside in their
former homes. Until further notice, that was. The wise
men settled nothing; simply advocated a waiting policy.
That night bets were laid among the younger generation,
a graceless set of jokers who never took anything seriously, that the Chief's wives would remain so.

The situation remained uncertain for a very long time.
Indeed, there is legitimate doubt as to whether it was ever
cleared up. The bulk of the population made a serious
mistake. They reckoned without Le Guen's zealous
obstinacy over his convert. The priest had his weather eye
open for squalls and was tipped off about the latest turn
of events by Ezoum the Catechist. He went at once to
the Chief and deployed all his Roman Catholic powers
of persuasion for the old villain's benefit. Both sides
imagined theirs to have been the decisive role. Fundamental lack of understanding caused each faction to
under-estimate the other.

It was a very long time since the Essazam people had
been really angry. Angry enough, that was, to make the
whole country, including the missionaries and colonial
Administration, feel nervous. Lack of trouble had allowed
people to forget the recent history of these simple folk.
There they were, scratching a precarious living from a

country which was a haven of primitive customs and economic backwardness. Since the restoration of Chief Essomba Mendouga no one disputed their rights or was ill-disposed towards them. As far as the Reverend Father Le Guen was concerned, they possibly imagined he had settled in Essazam out of love of the country.

Le Guen himself knew only one side of their character. His experience of the tribe was restricted to the years of peace. He had no idea how they could hold out against anything alien or behave when their peace of mind was disturbed.

On this fateful night Le Guen set the Chief effectively upon his private road to Damascus, leaving the wise men under the impression that they had established an armistice. Next morning things took a sensational turn. The Chief announced that he would not hear a word against his decision. He had sent his wives back to their clans. He had no intention of allowing talk about going back on his word.

This time the wives really had had enough. They began to leave in ones and twos, carrying their worldly possessions in wicker baskets. They straggled all round the village saying goodbye to people. Some cried—or did their best to squeeze out a few tears—others could not conceal their distress at leaving. This had been their village for many years. It was where their friends and relatives lived. These were the fields they had so often tilled. The ones with children were the most pitiable. Heart-rending little scenes went on everywhere and Chris tactfully took his aunt out of the way of it all.

These departures had repercussions. Several of the distinguished visitors who had come because of the Chief's illness departed in a huff. They decided that the repudiation of a woman belonging to their own clan was a personal insult. Therefore their presence was superfluous.

Makrita was the only one who took up a stand. She remained behind, denying hotly that her house was not her own property; maintaining eloquently that she belonged permanently both to the Ebazok clan and to the village of Essazam itself; saying it was nonsense to suppose that the Chief was not her husband for keeps.

His eldest wife had mastered her initial incoherence. She was playing the finest role of her entire career, her feelings well controlled. She was starting from scratch to get restoration of her conjugal rights.

First she summoned those members of her clan who had turned up in Essazam during the Chief's illness. She professed to be in need of their advice. These were not conservative old reactionaries, but up-and-coming young men. The Ebibots, for example, were famous for always getting their own way. They had faith in brisk self-assertion and forceful argument. More important, they adored Makrita to the point of idolatry. They possibly felt the affront to her more keenly than she did herself.

These quick-tempered young men distrusted the tribal sages; they despised their inconclusive palavering for the sake of maintaining the *status quo*! They quickly pointed out to Makrita that her real enemy was Le Guen. She should have aimed at him right from the beginning. This White man, and no one else, had bewitched the Chief with his sorcery. Why had Le Guen brought him back from the dead? (All the Essazam were convinced that the administration of Extreme Unction had re-animated the Chief's corpse.) Was it not done to impress the whole tribe with their Chief's conversion? To pack the Church with faithful worshippers? He saw the Chief daily for as long as he wished. Doubtless Le Guen must exercise the most profound influence.

They were well aware of the risks they would run in openly declaring war on Le Guen. Theirs was the constant fear that Authority would take bloody reprisals against the tribe. This had been done on every previous occasion when a missionary was the victim of violence. Accordingly they decided upon more subtle methods. Here opinions became divided. Despite separate discussions they had still not put forward any suggestion of material benefit to Makrita's plans.

Shortly before noon on this particular day Le Guen was happily trying out the new harmonium, brought back after his visit to the Bishop. Though this instrument had been acquired for the village by subscription, Le Guen's superior had only let him have it on certain conditions. The most important was, for him to abandon or modify his present methods of proselytising. In the opinion of higher authority these were not sufficiently tough, in the face of material counter-attractions. This creed of gain was already looming over Africa like a plague of locusts. Le Guen played on; nearby the boy listened enraptured to the soft chords. From time to time Le Guen bent across to him, asking whether he was enjoying the music. Waking as though from some ecstatic trance, the boy was full of excited enthusiasm. He stuttered that he had never heard anything so lovely. Compared with this instrument, the first one they had had, the little one, was only fit to be chopped up for firewood.

Though Makrita stole up the steps of the dais as noiselessly as a cat, Gustave was aware of her long before she reached them. Her harsh, set expression made him jump. He clung nervously to Le Guen's shoulder. When the priest asked what was the matter, he remained dumb with shock.

"Praise be to Jesus Christ!" the woman exclaimed in a deep, cavernous voice and strode towards Le Guen with measured steps. He carefully refrained from turning. He was anxious to give an impression of relaxed self-assurance. He had been expecting this visit for a long time now and dreading the thought of having to justify himself in her eyes.

"Can I make my confession, Father Le Guen?" the woman continued, in the same tone of voice. "Immediately, Father Le Guen," she added.

"Certainly, Makrita. Go and prepare yourself. I'll be with you in a moment."

When she turned her back and began to descend the steps again, the boy pulled a wry face at Le Guen. Le Guen grimaced back. The boy remained on the platform, hidden behind the harmonium, enjoying a gallery view down into the confessional-box. He was, however, too far away to hear anything. That was, so long as it was a case of whispering sins. In the present case this was of short duration, a fact which confirmed his apprehensive foreboding.

When Le Guen bent down to the grille and told Makrita he was ready, she behaved somewhat unexpectedly. Instead of reciting the ejaculatory prayer which preceded the actual confession, she simply coughed and cleared her throat a number of times. This left Le Guen greatly puzzled; the boy bemused.

"Father," she said, at last, in a ringing voice hardly suitable for the confessional, "Father Le Guen, I have been a Christian for more than twenty years; twenty years during which I have kept the Commandments of God and His Church. Nor is this all. For twenty years I have paid my dues and a good deal more. In twenty years I have never missed a Mass on the first Friday of every month— much less on any Sunday. For twenty years I have kept Easter as a Christian should—Father Le Guen, tell me what it is you find fault with in my conduct? I beg you to tell me."

"There is nothing that I have found fault with in you, my daughter," Le Guen replied. "What makes you think such a thought ever entered my head? On the contrary——"

Makrita cut him short. "You find no fault with me, you say, yet you have taken sides against me! And for whose sake? A slip of a girl who has never even learnt how to cross herself! A child of the Devil who's never been to Communion! A creature whom you don't even know! Do you have to practise ingratitude just because you're White and a European? Think of all the favours I've done you. All the eggs, pineapples, bananas, chickens, sheep and goats you've had from me—remember? Think of all the children I've rounded up from every corner of the district to attend your school, the poor little creatures! Think of all the folk I've talked into letting themselves be converted. Those who've received baptism at your hands, Father Le Guen! You ought to have a little more thought for your real friends——"

"But Makrita, my daughter, I have never taken sides with her—or against you."

"Well, what *have* you done, then?"

"I have allowed the Chief a completely free choice of the woman he loved——"

"And I suppose that means he didn't love me? Go on, say it—say I'm no beauty any more! What has she got that I haven't? I am beautiful too—do you hear me, Father Le Guen? *I'm beautiful.* You could easily convince the Chief of that if you wanted to. I'm beautiful—truly beautiful! I haven't changed. I'm still the same woman I always was, the woman he was after in the old days almost as soon as it was dark. I haven't changed since then. *Why doesn't he try me and see?*"

When he heard Makrita carrying on in this way, the boy scurried off for reinforcements in the shape of the cook. By the time they returned, Makrita had begun to sob convulsively, gasping out between each spasm: "I'm still beautiful, Father Le Guen—you could convince the Chief of that, I know you could——"

"Come, come, my child," Le Guen was saying, "I can't do such a thing: I haven't the right to meddle in matters of that sort."

"But it's your duty to stand by a Christian," Makrita replied. Her tears dried. A shrill edge to her voice denoted scandal in the offing. "Your duty is to protect a Christian soul—especially when a pagan, a child of Satan, tries to evict her!"

"Listen to me, Makrita. You are both children of God, without distinction. You are both *my* children."

"What? Her also, when she doesn't even know how to cross herself?"

"She will soon be baptised. You know that perfectly well."

"Ah! That's it, is it?"

The cook and the boy saw her suddenly straighten up in a single movement. The long, stiff, stick-like creature swept in silence out of the confessional. She skirted the wall with what can only be described as a *vengeful* stride and went out of the church without even crossing herself.

Although it was now late in the evening, she sent her eldest son to the headquarters of the clan with clear-cut instructions. Her little ruse had failed—she thought of her approach to Le Guen as a 'ruse'; now she was forced to adopt extreme methods.

Quite early in the morning two days later almost every male member of the Ebibot clan descended vengefully upon Essazam. They uttered extravagant expressions of hostility and made no secret of their bellicose intentions. They competed in denouncing the Chief's insult to their fellow-clanswoman. He was accused of having defied tradition by breaking his solemn word. In giving him this woman in marriage, they argued, had they not also made a life-alliance with him, sealed and reinforced by the birth of Maurice and Cecilia? Their kinswoman was the victim of a conspiracy and they would stop at nothing to re-establish her rights.

Not least depressing was the irony of the situation. At the time of the Chief's marriage to the girl later known as Makrita, all these young people were children. Some indeed were not even born. Not one of them recalled the circumstances of the event. When they talked of life-alliances, conspiracies, unalterable rights, they were simply using grand phrases. They did not believe in the ideas these words expressed. They did not even believe in the underlying customs. They mocked the concept, yet clung to the formula. In their eyes everything could be reduced to the terms of a game. Life itself they saw as a kind of high-class joke. These characters were not inspired by the slightest respect for humanity as such. Even force made only a very moderate impression upon them, because they never quite took its measure. Unperceptive to danger, they had no notion of fear. The Ebibots would have cheerfully declared massed war on the Gods themselves.

According to the fabricated legend which explained their customs, they were descended from a high-tempered man who had left Essazam after surviving a fight to the death with his own father. This in itself already made them accursed. He had gone far away to found a colony —to the other end of the world, the Essazam used to say, though in fact it was only seventy miles or so. They lacked both men and women to populate their colony and till the fields, so this fellow had collected what few friends he possessed, and turned them into brigands. Covered all over with dead leaves, their faces painted in the most bizarre fashion, they suddenly would appear, as from nowhere, in well-populated villages, raiding by night for male and female prisoners. They were specially on the look-out for young girls just past the age of puberty; these they subsequently forced to be their wives. Such incursions produced waves of panic and an occasional mass exodus. Finally the communities lying between Essazam and the new colony were practically disseminated. At a later date the Essazam tribe spread out over the deserted countryside and joined up with them, enlarging their territory in a most unexpected fashion. The Ebibots had now regained their old tribal centre.

They made it a point of honour to preserve intact those traditions of violence, duplicity and rapine which had originally gained them notoriety. Ragged, brawling, generally drunk, the most scarifying obscenities constantly upon their lips—such was the rag-tag army on which Makrita relied to recover her lawful spouse. The mere appearance of this army mortified her. She had very little choice in the matter. She consoled herself by bribing Ondoua and Ndibidi, the two most gluttonous old men in the tribe. She had no trouble in winning them over to her viewpoint, nor in convincing them as to the best means of dealing with the conflict.

Her numerous set-backs, far from exhausting her, on the contrary seemed actually to have increased her audacity, ambition, cruelty, persecution mania and ingrained hate and distrust of other people. She looked taller, scrawnier, more stick-like and unprepossessing than ever. She also found herself afflicted with a new physical ailment. Her voice, hitherto completely sexless, had suddenly broken into a gruff baritone. Malicious local gossips nicknamed her Old Man Makrita. They strongly supported her refusal to budge. Their idea was that she should be considered one of the local patriarchs; a permanent fixture both in the Ebazok clan and the village of Essazam. A solution which would, they reckoned, remedy the dispute.

The news of what was going on quickly percolated to other clans. What they heard, after the usual distortions had crept in, was that the Ebibots had re-established their kinswoman in her house by main force. The rest of the clans whose kinswomen had been repudiated in similar fashion now claimed that *their* good name was at stake. They charged into the district to re-establish the ladies concerned in their huts. The influx included several clans who had never had a good name anyway, but who saw this as an ideal opportunity to effect a smart *coup* on the cheap.

Worse was to come. Anaba, being the fortunate spouse-elect, the one and only wife whom the Chief proposed to marry in the eyes of God, was informed of the favour bestowed on her; clearly a legitimate choice, and indeed, considering the young lady's virtues and remarkable beauty, a natural one. Nevertheless it aroused murderous jealousy among the other rejected wives who, Anaba's clansmen heard, had brought their own male relatives out in force with the object of evicting Anaba. The result was that an indescribable horde of men, women, children and old folk poured into Essazam and camped on the edge of the village. They did this not only as a threatening gesture, but for a more compelling reason. The village was so full that there was no lodging for these new arrivals. So Essazam was transformed into a vast tribal battlefield, where the various clans were patiently manoeuvring into position like so many hostile armies, only awaiting the signal before they joined battle and began to tear one another to pieces.

Needless to say, the reappearance of Chris and his aunt had not gone unnoticed. When his friend, Bitama, came to see him, Chris was fast asleep. Bitama took it upon himself to shake the sleeper roughly awake. Chris had always found waking up a difficult business. On this particular day he surpassed himself. Bitama needed all the perseverance he later showed as a fifth-form classical scholar to wrench poor Chris from the arms of Morpheus. Finally he sat up with a jerk, rubbing his eyes, wrinkling his nose and pulling the most hideous faces, while Bitama stood there laughing. His brain still half-fogged, Chris sluiced himself with cold water from the jug, even going so far as to plunge his head into the bowl.

"No one," Bitama observed during this operation, "could say you're not a heavy sleeper, old boy."

"Wha? Whassat you nattering about?" demanded Chris, breaking off his hearty ablutions and raising a pair of watery eyes to meet those of his friend. "Ah, for Pete's sake, what an interfering bastard you are! Couldn't you let me sleep in peace? What's the matter, then? Been bitten by a horse-fly?"

"Sure, sure—a damned great tsetse. And you reckon you're a pretty fly boy yourself, don't you? Is this the way you part from an old friend, without so much as a goodbye? I suppose you fancy yourself as an Englishman now, or something——"

"What? *What?* You really are a prize bore, boy, that's the truth. What do you want with me today? More cosy chat about the P.P.P.? What bloody business is it of yours whether I go or stay, huh?"

Bitama went on laughing so heartily that Chris finally calmed down. Now he was properly awake he had no intention of behaving tiresomely himself. Presently he began to laugh too and this started Bitama off again, with a burst of almost hysterical hilarity. Watching him, Chris decided he was not exactly his normal self: he was cheerful enough, but underneath the gaiety Chris detected a note of anxiety.

"So you're back again, are you?" Bitama said. "How did that happen? Come on, tell. I suppose someone let you know that the Ebibots had——"

"The *Ebibots?* What sort of an animal's that? I don't know a thing about it. As far as we were concerned, it was all quite simple. Auntie wouldn't have lasted long at our place, anyway. She never stopped crying for a single moment after we'd pulled out. It's a very ordinary story: everything and everybody in Essazam had let her down. Including Le Guen, if you can credit it. How that old eunuch gets himself so popular among the ladies is something I shall never understand as long as I live."

"Oh, he became a habit, like any other habit: they got so used to seeing him around the place, you know."

"A habit? More like a drug, if you ask me. The day he leaves town there'll be a good few tears shed."

"Weeping and gnashing of teeth, as he'd put it himself," Bitama said. "Anyway, why did you bring that up? *Is* he going soon?"

"What the f—— do I care? I'm more interested in my aunt at the moment. God, how stupid women can get! Look, the whole of my family were putting themselves out at our place to make Auntie feel at home. Not the slightest use: nothing but blub, blub, blub. Honestly, it made me feel really bad, you've no idea how she got under my skin. My God, what a do! 'Auntie, what's the matter?' they all said, 'what's wrong?' they said. She'd lost Essazam: that was the long and short of it. Nothing could console her for having been turfed out of the bloody dump —and God, *what* a dump! She'd been treated like a slave all the time she was there, humiliated, kicked about as though she were some mangy old mongrel bitch—it still made no difference. While all these shenanigans were going on, the news came that the other wives were back home again—no, don't ask me why, because I don't know. Then Auntie insisted on my bringing her back too and that's all there is to it."

"But what about your aunt's kinsmen? Where are they? Aren't they here?"

"The clan to which my mother and aunt belong has nothing to do with Essazam. That's why none of them have turned up. Well, not many of them, anyway: I brought Auntie back just the same."

"It's all most exciting, *I* think," Bitama exclaimed. "I wish my old man had taught me more about the working of the tribe, when I was younger."

"Don't kid yourself, brother. You've been pretty lucky, if you only knew it. They're not usually such good value. You'll see: one day soon it'll all be over and then you won't think they're amusing at all."

"Have you seen the crowd camping on the outskirts of the village?"

"Have I not!" Chris said. "There was a girl there who clouted me one in the eye. Madly funny! One of these days I'll have to square accounts with her."

"Oh, I know the girl you mean. Pretty kid, but a bit too excitable for my taste."

"Your taste and mine obviously don't agree. But then you've never had your oats——"

"What do you intend to do with her?" Bitama asked.

"Whatever I bloody please. Who the hell do you think you are? Le Guen? I shall do what I like with her, precisely what I like, neither more nor less."

"Listen, Chris, you can't treat her like dirt just because she's illiterate. All young girls deserve some respect, even when they're uneducated and a bit on the jungly side——"

"God," Chris said, sniggering, "what a lot of bookish crap you do talk! There comes a point, my poor friend, when you're in serious danger of being taken for a proper c——. Oh dear, I'm *so* sorry, that wasn't what I meant to say—you know I don't think anything like that, of *course* I was just pulling your leg—— But honestly, why do you think men and women were made the way they are?"

"All right: what would *you* say if some bloody corner-boy came and screwed that girl of yours, the one you're so struck on?"

Chris thought for a moment and then said: "Well done, boy. One up to you. All the same, I'd like to point out that *I'm* not a corner boy."

"Anyway," Bitama put in triumphantly, "there's nothing to show that she'll let you have her."

"So that's your opinion, is it? Want to bet?"

"Sure! Anything you like. But I'll tell you something, in confidence: these girls have a damn sight more dignity than you'd think. Ah well: you'll find out for yourself. By the way, there's one of those boys down there you've managed to make an enemy of for life. You know, that chap who was at Kufra——"

"Oh yes, Raphael."

"He says he's going to teach you a lesson; he can't talk about anything else."

"What sort of lesson?" Chris asked.

"I don't know. He says that if he wanted to he could fix you good and proper—catch you red-handed distilling alcohol, for a start. Then he'd rope you up like a young pig for market and cart you off to Ongola, where you'd be shoved into clink. That's what he said, anyway."

"That's what he thinks, you mean. All these chaps who fancy themselves as Service veterans are just a bunch of stool-pigeons. I'd better keep my eyes peeled next time."

"What do you mean? Are you going to start brewing up again?"

"Too true I am."

"Haven't you made enough money already?"

"No, I haven't. Not yet, anyway."

There were tremendous inroads being made into the herds of smaller livestock round about Essazam. Not a day passed but some poor beast was poleaxed, its meat used to appease the resentful appetites of the invading clansmen. Yet the more trouble that was taken on their behalf, the more difficult they got. They were always complaining and demanding more, like treacherous conquerors who disregard the terms of a peace-treaty. On the other hand, every evening there was an amicable meeting between the elders of the whole tribe, who fraternised as wise men should and worked out various compromises to avert a real tribal disaster.

The last Sunday of August dawned clear and bright. The sun rose early, in a fine chorus of birdsong: everything and everybody that could put on their Sunday finery seemed to have passed the word. The world was a pattern of brilliant colours that glowed, sparkled, shimmered, flashing back and forth in friendly fashion, like two old acquaintances clapping each other on the back. It was a fairyland scene to stir the heart. Bitama said that this was the one day he would really remember from the whole of his adolescence. As he remained an incorrigible romantic, he used to add that it must have marked the last day of his childhood.

Years afterwards, in that little university town where he was to have so many strange experiences, he still maintained that everything went back to that bright Sunday of August 1948. Just as in retrospect every event that took place anywhere on that day seemed to push him forward into his future—even that solo flight by a man called Parker in—now what was the name of his plane? *Mohawk*, perhaps? And yet, could there have been anything with less relevance to the day as he actually experienced it?

He will content himself for the moment by returning in memory to the thickly wooded bank of the river and the thin, small crying of the birds as they flew away from it. The process of recollection engendered a somewhat morbid nostalgia. He liked to recall the unspeakable weariness which had racked him for weeks: above all, the silent feeling of misery that was his. Still on occasion he could re-experience it, though not in its full awfulness. A tune, a scent, or some other equally insignificant detail sufficed. He never managed to rid himself completely of this obsession, though he always said that the girl was not worth so much fuss.

What Chris had told him that evening in a burst of confidence was true. He had found her something special. People in his position often shot a line. There were millions of girls just like her, all over the world, Bitama thought; none of them of the least importance. "Why should she be the one who makes me so jealous?"

He watched the rest of that day's events like a spectator at some lengthy, drawn-out play. Twenty-four hours earlier life had filled him with heady excitement. It was as though he had aged several decades overnight.

Early in the morning Le Guen (doubtless with the Chief's connivance) spread the report that the Chief, in his unshakable desire to become a member of the Church Militant of Christ, preferred exile to a return to polygamy, with risk of dying suddenly in a state of Mortal Sin. This announcement produced a panic throughout that most respectable body, the wise men and elders of Essazam. Or, as Bitama thought of them, those pathetic old orangoutangs who had reduced public debate to futility.

On his return from the river-bank, still infatuated by the vision he had experienced, he found himself mingling with members of the Ekabmeyong clan, the one to which Anaba and the girl in question belonged. He noticed they were yawning and bored. At a loss for occupation, someone thought of wrestling, then Essazam's national sport. Immediately all the young men drifted towards the centre of the big village square, where the soft ground and plentiful dust would break a fall more easily. They gathered in a circle forming a kind of makeshift arena, where two men would square up to each other aggressively, push their long naked arms under each other's armpits, grip their opponent in a bear-like hug as thought about to kiss him, break loose, chuck themselves all over the place, execute cross-buttock throws and other such fancy tricks, till one of them had the other's shoulders actually touching the ground and won the match.

Very soon various young men from other clans came up, chests puffed out, rolling up their tattered trousers or loin-cloths above their thighs, and asked permission to enter the lists. This was readily granted.

The only people who turned up their noses at the contests were the young men of the Ebibot clan. Followed by a bunch of curious spectators and one or two aged village sorceresses and Bitama, who sensed something in the wind, they made their way to the Catholic Mission. They infiltrated right into the church along with the faithful bound for High Mass. On the face of it, there was nothing very edifying about their intentions. They remained seated during the whole of the first part of the service, snorting with laughter as they watched the genuine worshippers now standing, now sitting and now down on their knees. The time came for the sermon. After the reading of the first Lesson they pinched one another, so that those who had drowsed off woke up again, rubbed their eyes and listened.

Le Guen climbed into the pulpit while this was going on; he stood there, high above the congregation, stroking his beard thoughtfully. Then the candle-light, flickering over his features, revealed a sudden change of expression: the severe lines melted into a picture of amiable compassion. That was how Bitama described it afterwards. Le Guen began his sermon.

"It has occurred to me that when our beloved Yosifa— that fine Christian, that incomparable mother, that great-hearted woman—administered baptism to her son, our Chief, she forgot to give him a Christian name——"

One or two people laughed out loud at this. The whole church was filled with rustlings, coughs and whispered comments. This was the moment all the Essazam, Christians and pagans alike, had impatiently been awaiting.

Indeed it was the only reason why many of them had come. It was thus that the most important news had always been broken to them—the declaration of war, the invasion of France. Everyone remembered Le Guen's sermon on this occasion, a call for vengeance on the aggressor, delivered in a voice that fairly shook with passion. They had heard about the landing of the Allies in this way; about Hitler's death, which had aroused much controversy; about the abolition of the forced-labour battalions. To tell the truth, the last-named institution had not proved too irksome for the Essazam. They were fierce, jungle people and almost impossible to catch once they had vanished.

On this particular Sunday, the last in August of a year in the twentieth century of little importance and soon to be forgotten, the Essazam people of every creed gathered to hear about the miracle by which their Chief had been restored to life.

Le Guen was not a complete simpleton. He knew exactly what they were expecting of him and just what he needed to say in order to make hundreds, perhaps thousands, of conversions. After spending the whole of the previous night strengthening his resolve, he had finally made up his mind to say it. He had sworn before the Crucified Christ that even though such an act might offend his ingrained sense of propriety, he would nonetheless endure the violence done to his feelings. In this accursed century God's apostles had only a little time left to them: what excuse would he have for neglecting such an opportunity? Providence was certainly responsible, even if he personally had placed no faith in the so-called miracle. For the first time he was about to apply just those methods of expediency which the Bishop had advocated.

"Oh, it's not a serious matter," he resumed, in a cheerfully affable voice and with that easy command of Essazam idiom and dialect which he, alone among the European residents, managed to achieve. "It's not serious at all. The only reason I mentioned it at all was to announce to you the name our Chief has taken. His new name as a member of the community of the faithful in Christ. That name is—Lazarus."

The word at once caused a considerable stir. Le Guen had to wait for quite a time before all was still once more. He was quite relaxed—or making a very great effort to appear so. As he stood in the pulpit he presented his usual Sunday appearance, complete with gestures, tics and style of delivery. His whole congregation assumed him to be going through a spiritual crisis. He now launched into a long, rambling sermon. When it was over he realised, with mixed pride and puzzlement, that he had not made explicit reference to the miracle in connection with the Chief. He had simply contrived, by discussing the story of Lazarus and the Chief's illness almost in the same breath, to establish a link between them in people's minds. There was no coercion about it: merely suggestion.

At one point in his sermon Le Guen exclaimed, somewhat pathetically: "But why, why should certain people wish to spoil the joy which we feel today when Lazarus is risen again?" This remark was occasioned by the interruptions of a tight little knot of young men strategically placed in the congregation. First they whispered to each other, then jeered out loud. Stopping his discourse the better to observe them, the priest recognised them as members of the Ebibot clan. It became apparent to him that their acceptance of the ideas expressed in his sermon was unenthusiastic.

"Why," he persisted, "should certain people, spurred on by Satan, labour to set themselves against the ways which God in His Mercy has marked out for his humble creatures to walk in?"

At this point Azombo, the Achilles among these young men, could stand it no longer. He emitted a loud groan of protest. He was very like Achilles, with the same wild courage, ardour, quickness of temper and thunderous rages. This gesture caused a flutter throughout the church. All the small children began to giggle helplessly, scared and delighted that a mere ordinary man had dared interrupt Le Guen in the pulpit. Determined to face up to these feather-brained youths, Le Guen leaned over the edge of the pulpit and brandished a forefinger at them.

"Take care," he thundered, "take care that through your errors, foolishnesses, pride and stubbornness some irreparable misfortune does not come upon the tribe! I bid you take care, young men!"

"Why can't you mind your own business?" roared Azombo. "Why do you have to come sticking your long nose into our affairs?"

"I have *not* meddled with your affairs, young man," Le Guen rapped back, allowing himself to slip into the rôle of accused person.

Le Guen and Azombo launched into a first-class row. The priest stabbed away more threateningly than ever with his forefinger, while his adversary shook a frenzied fist at the pulpit, waving his arm to and fro like a pendulum. It was at this point that Ezoum the Catechist, who acted as sidesman every Sunday, decided to act the brief part forced upon him by a lifetime of sexual repression and servility. He moved briskly up behind the young Ebibots, swishing the enormous cane he carried to draw their attention. He put his finger to his lips in an attempt to silence Azombo and end the row. The congregation was struck dumb with amazement at the novelty of the occasion. Perplexed, they listened to the arguments from both sides, both seemingly convincing.

Ezoum's action did him very little good. The situation suited Azombo admirably; circumstances had put him into a position where he felt wholly at his ease. One word from this dark Achilles was enough. His Myrmidons threw themselves at the intruder, laid him flat in the dust, jumped on him and submitted his person to further painful indignities. He only escaped thanks to Le Guen, who clambered down hastily from his pulpit and managed to calm the infuriated young men by magnanimously suggesting that they should come and talk the whole thing over with him after Mass. Though they havered a little over making a pact of any sort with Makrita's mortal enemy, which was how Le Guen's proposition appeared to them, they nevertheless agreed. Beating up Ezoum had drawn off the worst of their anger. They even consented to leave the church, so that Le Guen could resume the celebration of the Mass where he had abandoned it. He made no attempt to finish his sermon. His inspiration had departed.

The subsequent discussion between the Ebibot youths and Le Guen only served to add fuel to the flames. The youths wanted Le Guen to renounce his ascendancy over the Chief, and not force him into monogamy, unless his intention were to marry Makrita. Le Guen restricted himself to a declaration that it was his bounden duty to further the Kingdom of Christ. He even besought them to let him baptise them—a pleasantry which led the youths to break off the discussion.

However, this was for the moment only. After they had come out fuming from the missionary's study into the courtyard, they put their heads together. Back they came, all smiles now: what fear had outweighed the desire to wring his neck, Le Guen wondered. He listened patiently while they outlined their proposals for a sort of compromise. They wanted the whole thing finished as soon as possible, they told him, so that they could return to their own part of the country. These rough simple peasants had a deep-seated passion for their native soil.

The Chief, they suggested, should marry little Anaba in church, since he insisted upon it. Thus he would make her his wife in the eyes of God, but his other wives should remain in Essazam. It was their village and no one could seriously consider uprooting them.

"I hope you enjoy making up these fairy-stories," Le Guen said. He saw very clearly the ambiguity and wiliness of such a proposition. "I have no doubt you can imagine a man living virtuously in the close neighbourhood of women who yesterday were his wives and would very much like to remain his wives. I know what I'm talking about. I've some experience of such matters. What do you suppose will really happen? It only needs a suitable occasion, a fleeting twinge of desire and the man is in grave danger of relapsing into mortal sin, isn't he?"

"You mean of going to bed with one of his wives?" queried Azombo, who liked everything clear.

"Yes."

"And what difference could that possibly make?" Azombo exclaimed. "What on earth does it matter if he does it once or twice on the side, Father? Don't the Christians ever go to bed with women who aren't their wives in the eyes of God?"

Le Guen came to the conclusion that his words had fallen on barren soil too long and took his leave of the young men.

The clock above the Mission House was striking midday as the Ebibots returned to Essazam. They were aggrieved at their failure with Le Guen and doubtful what they should do to free themselves from their duty to Makrita and return home. Singly rather than *en masse*, unwilling and ashamed, they resigned themselves to joining in the wrestling matches. Each in turn came forward and asked permission to enter the ring. Every time, despite the reputation this clan enjoyed, permission was granted. Very soon they demonstrated that they were still top dogs. Azombo was champion. He laid the other victors of the clans flat on their backs. The competitors gave up individual bouts, measuring up to each other in teams—which meant, in effect, clans. Even after the Ebibot intrusion, there was not a breath of violent partisanship about the competition. In a perfectly natural, unselfconscious way, the participants were wildly enthusiastic: wrestling was one of their greatest pleasures.

Among the young girls a somewhat different atmosphere prevailed.

Those of the Ekabmeyong clan, in emulation of their brothers' inventive spirit, decided to ward off Sunday boredom by performing a certain dance, then all the rage among the women of Essazam. They arranged themselves in a large circle. One girl stood in the middle, jigging, shimmying and intoning the words to a simple, if monotonous, refrain. The rest clapped in time to the rhythm, joined excitedly in the chorus and uttered little yodelling cries which gradually worked them up to a fine pitch.

The girls of the other clans—even the Ebibots, whose reputation as nagging shrews matched their brothers' for general bloody-mindedness—put on their most enchanting smiles and had no trouble persuading their Ekabmeyong sisters to let them join in. The latter group were most accommodating. At least until Medzo, Anaba's younger sister, arrived on the scene. To Medzo fell the honour of bringing the situation to a head.

3

AT the time of the events this story describes, the girl was barely fifteen. An impetuous, passionate crea-ture, *la belle* Medzo, her opulent bosom the more striking for the bird-fine adolescent body. Already the most attractive woman in the place, she had never been caught behaving in that calculating way philosophers through the ages have claimed as a distinguishing feature of the human species. She did not walk : she ran or skipped like a young antelope. Instead of talking, she was all ex-clamations. Smiles and melancholy nostalgia were not for her; when she laughed, she nearly exploded. Tears she despised and only really let herself go during her frequent transports of rage. Medzo enjoyed an uneasy popularity in the bosom of her clan. Her kinsfolk were resigned to her ways much as peasants resign themselves to a tornado after a long drought. Those who knew her said that she had lost her innocence almost the moment she was born. Medzo had indeed been the object of more than one gallant, if premature assault—generally at the hands of some enthusiastic visiting trader, many of whom came through during the cocoa season. On these occasions she had defended herself like a wildcat. Not to preserve her virtue—upon which the Essazam placed relatively little value—but simply following spontaneous instinct. In all the diverse situations life threw up, the only reaction she knew was to fight. To rape Medzo was beyond the powers of any normal male.

She had arrived with the rest of the clan and chose to

camp with them outside the village rather than live in her sister's house. On the morning of this last Sunday in August she rose early, as was her custom. She made her way to the nearby river-bank to fetch water. The clan had dragged along large numbers of babies and small children : the water was to wash them.

Bitama had no idea what might have led up to the girl's meeting and making love to Chris. Both he and the other boy had spent the night at Chris's aunt's house. Chris, presumably, must have risen early too, as he usually did, and then spent a long time squatting on his aunt's verandah, another regular habit, scratching his legs, a habit which Bitama found extremely irritating. Chris's thighs were permanently scarred with criss-cross nail-marks.

All the girl had to do was to follow her usual route to the creek. The path she took passed in front of the hut of Chris's aunt. He must have seen Medzo pass and followed her, Bitama thought. Chris would have caught up with her at the point where the track entered a dense patch of bush, hiding them from inquisitive eyes in the village. That was where Chris must have made his advances to the girl.

Like all idealistic young men who start with an idyllic concept of Woman and are therefore feminists, Bitama had now swung over to an opposite condition. A few short hours ago he would have hotly repudiated the idea of the brutish coupling he had since accidentally witnessed. Accordingly he relegated Woman to the category of mere Female Animal and managed to persuade himself that anyone could get *that* from her, simply by asking. It did not occur to him that Chris and Medzo might have been carrying on their affair for several days before it culminated in the way he observed. He would have been shocked and scared by the complex web of mutual longings, secret meetings, erotic urges and lovers' promises existing in every society to help people flout that society's official code. Intellectually precocious, though unaware that he was, Bitama was emotionally and sexually retarded. Medzo was responsible for his first genuine spasm of physical frustration. This was rendered the more agonising by his unconscious refusal to recognise that such physical instincts were important *per se*. He persistently regarded them as of a secondary nature. He was like a man sitting on his doorstep with the house ablaze behind him and obstinately arguing against the destructive powers of fire.

When Bitama woke and found that Chris was nowhere to be seen, he decided the creek was the likeliest place to search. Chris bathed there every morning. So off Bitama went down that fatal path and came upon them somewhere after the third or fourth bend. There they were in the dewy dawn, locked like a pair of wrestlers, scratching and clawing at each other—yet by no means in anger. They had not even bothered to lie down; they were coupling on their feet, with unbelievable passion and violence.

If there was one thing upon which he congratulated himself afterwards and which built up his self-esteem, it was the fact that he did not cry out, or impede the progress of what he poetically described as "the Irreparable Act". He hid himself not far away. In any case they were too occupied to notice him. He watched. He reflected later that what he saw finally made a man of him: Such remarks had no meaning outside Bitama's private thoughts.

When he saw Medzo in the village later that morning, there *was* a faint air of excitement about her. Even so it remained barely perceptible, since it differed little from her normal vivacity.

Medzo did not finish her usual domestic tasks till about one o'clock. Then she paid a call on her sister, laughing and cheerful, and said: "Come and dance with us, lovey.

You must be bored to death, all alone here in this huge house."

"Don't you realise I'm pregnant?" Anaba replied, gently. "I mustn't overstrain myself."

"As though you were the first woman ever to carry a child in your belly! Look, darling, your noble embryo won't come to any harm. As for overstraining yourself, all you'll have to do is clap your hands, for God's sake. Ah, come on—come and dance with us, h'm?"

Anaba was weak where her younger sister was concerned. This wild hoyden got her way with practically everyone in the Ekabmeyong clan. Anaba allowed herself to be persuaded and the two sisters went off together to where the dancing was going on. With a fine contempt for priorities, Medzo marched straight into the middle of the ring, practically throwing out the girl who happened to be there at the time. Then she began to improvise. She was blissfully happy, floating in a haze, fresh from the discovery of her full womanhood. Fluently she threaded verse after verse together: her facility and relaxed grace aroused the admiration and astonishment of the whole circle. Medzo was attacking her sister's rivals, together with their clans and even their children. An endless stream of sarcasm, insults and defiant invective flowed from her lips:

O you who hear my words, sisters of mine,
Tell me, sisters, what names can our tongue command
For women such as these, lizards with crooked claws,
Women who, though dishonoured, rejected and disowned,
Still hang around, still cling and grovel and beg?
Tell me, sisters, you who hear my words,
Are not such women as these—
Women who, though dishonoured, rejected and disowned,
Still hang around, still cling and grovel and beg—
Are they not fit to be called

Limed twigs, gluepots? Such sticky tags suit them well.
O you who hear my words, dear sisters of mine,
To think how they cling and grovel, though they have
  been disowned!
Ah weep for this miserable soul, most simple and
  innocent!
Weep for him, worthy man, poor bird limed in this snare!
What plight is his, struggling, weeping, crying,
Calling on God, his mother, the ghosts of his ancestors;
O you who hear my words, dear sisters, weep with him.
How will he ever free his limbs from the snare?
Weep and lament for him—

The Ekabmeyong girls applauded wildly. Those who belonged to the Ebazoks, being bound to observe strict neutrality as hosts, merely acclaimed her with enthusiastic laughter. This, of course, could be taken as a simple tribute to her stunning talents. Those from the other clans, after some fluttering indecision and whispered consultation amongst themselves, displayed a certain hostility. Timid at first, their show of resentment swelled as Medzo, who looked like going on for weeks, continued systematically to flay those unfortunate women *who, though dishonoured, rejected and disowned, still hung around, still clung and grovelled and begged.*

Suddenly an extraordinary cry went up; the kind of bestial moan-cum-shriek that an animal will give when trapped under falling masonry. This was the signal for a quite indescribable *mêlée*, during which Bitama had ample opportunity to feast his eyes on plump buttocks and private parts : the Essazam girls seldom wore panties, which on occasions such as this could prove distinctly embarrassing. Medzo herself managed to struggle clear and raced off to tell her kinsmen what was happening. They abandoned their wrestling match when they heard about the grave events at the other end of the square.

Especially when they gathered that their precious Anaba was involved and might become a casualty in her delicate condition. These men of the Ekabmeyong clan were sufficiently irked by the excessive number of wins their Ebibot opponents had scored. Medzo's news sent them charging, as one man, to the rescue—after all, it was to protect Anaba's interests that they had come in the first place—followed by the Ebibots, unsure what it was all about but bristling with aggressiveness and already in the mood to counter-attack against Ekabmeyong provocation.

The Ekabmeyong brigade were hard-pressed on two fronts. From behind they were attacked by the Ebibots, who had at last found an opportunity for exercising their particular kind of talent, and by the young men from various other clans, who had no idea what the quarrel was about, but asked nothing better than to weigh in on the stronger side: i.e. the Ebibots. Thus only with difficulty did the clan succeed in rescuing Anaba, who was dragged out from under a mass of struggling bodies, half unconscious, beaten black and blue, covered with bites; scratched and groaning as though about to die. They formed a square round her and escorted her to the Palace. Besides locking the poor girl safely away, they raised the alarm and created a state of general panic and confusion. Then they launched a massive counter-attack, men, women, and children together, throwing the weight of superior numbers into the scales of battle. "Don't-knows" from the other clans changed sides and joined in with them. The tide was now on the turn; slowly the Ebibots were forced back. Finally they broke and ran away in utter confusion, their attackers hard on their heels. Refuge was sought in the huts at the far end of the village.

The Ebibots were far from defeated. Their opponents were out of breath and hampered by the women and children in their ranks. When it came to staying-power, women and children were rather like a fire in a bale of straw—blazing one minute, out the next. So the Ebibots seized this golden opportunity to counter-attack most effectively. They forced the Ekabmeyong to seek refuge in such unseemly places as women's huts, where they could be heard knocking pots and pans over in their embarrassment. At the same time the floating auxiliaries changed sides again. They did not appear quite to grasp what was at stake in this vast battle or even what it was all about. This lunatic brawl went on, now one side, now the other gaining a temporary advantage.

The Chief himself came out from his Palace intending to restore law and order. Roar, curse and stamp as he would, he found it impossible to make himself heard, let alone cool the combatants' ardour. Le Guen, who had heard the news from Gustave, came hot-foot from the Catholic Mission and tried to intervene. By a train of events which he was powerless to avoid, he found himself embroiled in the actual fighting. While thus engaged, he received some very nasty knocks, mostly from the Ebibots; in particular from Azombo, who had by no means forgiven him for his attitude. Le Guen extricated himself as best he could, scuttled back to the Mission and took to his bed.

Joseph Schloegel wheeled the motorcycle-sidecar combination out of the garage. After considerable effort he managed to start it. As he hoisted himself into the saddle, streaming with sweat, he noticed that young Gustave had stowed himself away in the sidecar. He merely shrugged his shoulders, giving the poor boy a chance, for the first time in his short, wretched life, to have a furtive glimpse of the Big City. Brother Joseph's object in riding to Ongola at breakneck speed was to warn the authorities that the Essazam clans were cheerfully massacring each other. The riot, he informed them, had already claimed victims in

147

Le Guen and one of the Chief's wives; doubtless there would be others. Finally he emphasised that without external intervention, no one could tell how or when the combatants would stop fighting.

Meanwhile the crazy battle surged to and fro through the streets of Essazam. Victims were pursued, caught, thrown to the ground after a short struggle and beaten senseless. To begin with there had been some fine general strategy, but soon this gave way to complete chaos. Neat tactical movements degenerated into individual slogging-matches, graceless as they were inglorious. When these young Essazam tribesmen were wrestling, they had shown themselves not only loyal but also capable of real chivalry and courtesy. Now, however, they seemed to consider no holds barred.

The men fought on in the manner of rutting stags: they stood toe to toe and slammed it out, hitting each other in the belly, gouging their opponents' eyes, thumping and pounding away. When one man got in a blow, he stood like a fool and waited for his opposite number to hit back. When the expected attack came, he bore it phlegmatically, then took up the offensive himself, a bold grin on his face, and returned the compliment. To watch them one would have thought that the very idea of ducking or weaving was beyond their comprehension. They never let up till one or the other had come out as unquestioned victor, his opponent stretched out on his belly in the dust. Then he would grind the poor fellow's face against the ground once or twice, till he yelled for mercy. Even so, it frequently happened that the victor refused to give quarter to the man he had defeated.

The women floored each other by pulling their opponents' legs from under them. They would bend and crouch almost at ground level, then charge, head down. The one who first got a good grip on the other's leg would yank

148

it up in a sharp and violent movement, thus tipping the poor creature off balance. Over and over they would roll together, first one on top and then the other, each trying to stay there at least long enough to stuff her adversary's eyes, nose, ears and mouth full of dust.

The children followed the example of their elders, according to sex; little boys copied the men, little girls strove to emulate the women. Their behaviour differed from that of the grown-ups in one respect, however: quite often two children of opposite sex might be seen having a tremendous set-to, which they were liable to carry through to the bitter end. Nor were they fussy about the methods of in-fighting they employed, frequently going so far as to bite one another like mad dogs.

The Chief, aided by other members of his own clan, which remained neutral from start to finish, took advantage of the combatants' increasing exhaustion and finally put an end to the battle. This was a gruelling job. The man who bore the brunt of it was Raphael. With selfless courage he flung himself into the thick of the fight, dealing out lethal American-style uppercuts all round till he had both sides under control. Finally he shut the whole lot of them in various huts, taking care to separate them off according to clan. Little by little, peace and quiet returned to Essazam.

When the word went round that the forces of law and order had arrived, one or two miserable victims were still pursued by those with a rankling urge to settle old scores. But the convoy of jeeps and trucks, headlights blazing and packed with native troops carrying rifles, quickly put paid to any last lingering grudges. A moment later there was not a soul in sight.

Shortly afterwards Lequeux arrived on the scene, in personal command of the detachment. With him came Palmieri, who had not summoned up the courage to leave his young wife alone in Ongola. The military operation of encircling the village had been directed by a French sergeant. Under his guidance they went off to inspect the worst trouble-spots. Meanwhile a magnificent fifteen-hundredweight had drawn up; even in the darkness it was obviously shining and spotless. From it there emerged a number of African officials, laden with huge files and dossiers. At once these people marched off to the Palace. They did not ask the way, behaving with complete self-assurance. They demonstrated their familiarity with riotous insubordination and the proper treatment to mete out to those responsible.

After the Europeans had inspected and approved the sergeant's disposition of troops all round the village, they made their way to the Catholic Mission. Brother Joseph, who had just returned, conducted them to Le Guen's bedside. He had fallen asleep and was awoken by the sound of their footsteps. This influx of visitors into his room took him somewhat aback.

"Well, Father," said Lequeux, in a most kindly voice, "I hope you're feeling better now?"

"Oh, not too bad," Le Guen murmured, doing his best to smile and rubbing his eyes to hide his embarrassment. "Not too bad," he repeated, "not too bad at all." To allay the anxiety and solicitude on his visitors' faces he added, "I received one or two blows in the scuffle—I'm certain they were not in fact aimed at me——" Le Guen, quite certainly lying about this, emphasised his opinion strongly. "Anyway, none of them were fatal, it seems—and not, I think, even of any real seriousness——"

"*Fatal?* I should hope not. It would only have needed that to make a proper job of it."

"Please sit down," Le Guen said. "Please, do sit down, dear lady."

The missionary often received visitors in his bedroom, so there were plenty of chairs available. The only thing that kept him in bed was the fact that he had been caught undressed, as it were. This prevented him from exercising full hospitality.

Lequeux put on a severe expression. His lips vanished in a thin straight line; his demeanour was that of a stern father preparing to punish a son who has, for exceptional reasons, strayed from path of virtue.

"Perhaps you are ill?" Madame Palmieri suggested. "Do you need medical attention, Father?"

"I am most grateful for your thoughtfulness, Madame. But I have already had a professional opinion, you see. A friend of mine, a doctor, who dropped in—I mean, the medical officer who made himself responsible for the Chief——"

"I very much hope," Lequeux said softly, "I *very* much hope you will be able to recognise and identify those insolent creatures who had the unheard-of audacity to raise their filthy paws against a Frenchman."

"Listen to me," Le Guen said, half sitting up in bed and speaking quite calmly. "Do not take that line, if you please, *Monsieur le Chef de la région*. Here in Essazam, among provincials such as myself, there are no such things as 'Frenchmen' or 'insolent creatures'. There are only ourselves—that is, the Essazam——"

"Ah! Just so. The Essazam! And what then, pray? I've heard a great deal about you, Father Le Guen. Even more of your beliefs and ideas, which seem to me—how shall I put it?——"

"*Extravagant*, perhaps?" Le Guen suggested.

"With all due respect to your cloth, Father, yes. Extravagant is exactly the word I had in mind. I have been working among the Blacks even longer than you have. Do you catch *me* calling myself an Essazam, or any nonsense of that sort?"

"That, *Monsieur le Chef de la région*, is your affair."

"You are wrong, Father. I understand that in your profession it is necessary to place oneself as far as possible on the same level as the natives. That's reasonable enough, I suppose. But to go on from there quite seriously to want to pass for a native yourself—that's extravagant, *really* extravagant. Listen, Father: the real truth of the matter is that you are a Frenchman before all else——"

"If I might give you one piece of advice, *Monsieur le Chef de la région*, it would be this. Since you hold these opinions, leave us—and by us, I mean the Essazam— severely alone. That's all. What is the point of provoking us?"

"That's exactly what I want to know," put in Brother Joseph. "Things are quite *hot* enough as it is," he added, hoping that this feeble pleasantry would ease the atmosphere. "Come now, ladies and gentlemen. The Reverend Father would be grateful if you would let him dress. I feel quite sure he is fit enough to get up. You've been in worse jams than this before now, eh, Your Reverence?"

"I'm sorry, Brother Joseph," Le Guen said, lying back sadly on his pillows, "but I really do feel dreadfully tired. My one concern at the moment is that M. Lequeux should understand the exact trend of my thoughts. I am not disputing his prerogative of authority: far from it. But from my own point of view I cannot help seeing things in a different light. In any case, I repeat what I said earlier. Even though I had a sizeable drubbing, I'm certain the blows were not deliberately aimed at me. In one sense I did wrong to intervene at all, since this simply amounted to joining in the fray." Le Guen paused for a moment, then turned to Schloegel. "In point of fact, Brother Joseph, what does the whole business add up to? What's the damage?"

"Things are all right," Schloegel said. "Well, nothing serious, anyway. I simply can't get over it. A few trifling cuts and sprains, one or two eyes poked out: that's about the lot. Oh, one very unfortunate thing! The Chief's young wife had a miscarriage earlier this evening."

"That's wretched bad luck," Le Guen said.

"Damnation!" Lequeux suddenly exploded. "Why were there so many of them all assembled in this one village? *Why?*"

"Look," said Schloegel, whose patience was visibly fraying, "no one did all this *deliberately*. Can you get that into your head? Still, one shouldn't forget that a certain number of rather serious things have happened—extremely serious, in fact, as far as *they* are concerned——"

"Extremely serious for everybody, Brother Joseph," Le Guen corrected him, in a tired voice. "For us, too. Even for *Monsieur le Chef de la région*. Anything that is a serious matter for them—the illness of their tribal Chief, for instance—should also affect everyone else, including ourselves. If not, what in God's name do we suppose we're playing at here?"

"As far as I can understand," ventured Brother Joseph, still very humble and in a spirit of conciliation which did him great credit, "it was what might be described as a kind of collective nervous breakdown, wouldn't you agree?"

"A collective nervous breakdown; yes," Lequeux pronounced. "And an inevitable one, with so many men assembled in so confined a space. The trouble about such gatherings, whether more or less accidental or not, is that they form the springboard for revolt and insurrection——"

"Well, now, ladies and gentlemen, I think we ought to leave the Reverend Father to his well-earned rest, don't you?" Brother Joseph suddenly announced. He had guessed that Le Guen would not exactly appreciate the theories put forward by the Administrator-in-Chief to the Colonies. "Don't disturb yourself too much on account of that poor girl, Your Reverence," he said to Le Guen. "Your friend the doctor is taking good care of her. As far as I can tell, he isn't over-worried by her condition."

Lequeux and his party, accompanied by Joseph Schloe-gel, returned to the village where they joined the African officials in the Palace audience-chamber.

These had gone about their business with dispatch. In accordance with their usual procedure in such cases they had begun by advising the Chief to remain in his private apartments and not to interfere in any way. A tribal chief was never held personally responsible for any serious disturbances of which those under his jurisdiction might be found guilty.

There was still the job of finding the instigators of the riot: the actual ringleaders and other hotheads. To this end they had summoned all the people in the village regarded as "sensible" and "responsible". In effect, it meant all the old men. The administration had little inclination to take notice of the younger generation, which was a good deal too turbulent for their liking. Officialdom preferred to discredit and humiliate the young by ignoring their existence—except when clapping them in jail. So far everything had gone exactly according to precedent.

The whole scheme collapsed like a card-castle when the Essazam elders told these African officials that they would prefer to keep themselves to themselves. They had no inclination to wash their dirty linen in public with strangers. This line was in sharp contrast to the goodwill on which the officials had always been able to rely when visiting the other tribes. The elders of Essazam seemed backward and uncivilised, obviously averse to denouncing their kinsmen. Accordingly they discreetly withdrew to huts on the very outskirts of the village, betraying a non-co-operative spirit which, as far as the officials could recall, had been dormant for decades.

The disconcerted African officials could do nothing, when their two superior officers returned, except admit

154

rebuff. Lequeux now needed all his powers of decision and initiative to cope. He had but a few seconds for reflection. He had to find, and put into operation, a more suitable plan of campaign. The French sergeant was summoned and told to detail a small detachment for escort duty *Monsieur le Chef de la région* had decided personally to inspect the huts one by one, accompanied by his Private Secretary, Giovanni Palmieri, whose wife still did not budge an inch from his side; followed by his A.D.C., the French sergeant, and Brother Joseph, whose rôle in this manœuvre was a little vague. These distinguished people were surrounded by a strong escort, bristling with rifles and fixed bayonets. It was not difficult to imagine the shock that such a display made. Especially since the village was already encircled by the military.

When Lequeux entered the hut where Chris was, he at once smelt the agitator beneath the garb of the college student. His attire was in sharp contrast with the usual rags worn by jungle peasants, even though the cotton trousers were patched in several places and looked a sorry sight. Lequeux had an overpowering dislike of well-dressed young Negroes. They seemed to him to be aping European fashions in clothes and also, doubtless, the European spirit of freedom and easy manner. Such qualities in a native could easily turn into arrogance and disrespect for authority.

So he asked Chris, via the interpreter, who he was. Remaining seated Chris replied that he was born and bred in the district, upon which he was commanded to stand. After a moment's hesitation, Chris obeyed. Since his character was the exact opposite of a martyr's, he practised being self-effacing when confronted with a display of strength. More than ever convinced that he had to deal with a most undesirable character, Lequeux asked Chris further questions. How old was this local specimen? Had he any papers?

Chris pulled his student's identity card out of his pocket and gave it to them. Lequeux, Palmieri and even Palmieri's wife pounced on this document. Then Palmieri flung his arms round Chris's neck, and cheerfully began to fraternise with him, saying he was delighted to make the acquaintance of a scholar from the College of the Humanities and Modern Studies at Ongola. He added that even before this college had been translated into the famous Lycée Maréchal-Leclerc, it had acquired a very solid reputation for unruliness, lack of discipline, and systematic anarchy among the black students. His identity card was returned to him. Finally the visitors departed, after a whispered colloquy between Lequeux and his Private Secretary. Chris decided things were beginning to look rather black for him.

In various huts, the escort picked up one or two young men and took them to the audience-chamber in the Palace. As was expected this immediately brought out the whole tribe. Everyone who had taken part in the great quarrel turned up of his own accord, determined to demonstrate solidarity with those who had been arrested. They did not realise that these kinsmen of theirs had only been taken into custody as hostages, to force the remaining young men to come before *Monsieur le Chef de la région*. He was highly displeased at seeing his authority thus flouted. They flooded into the audience-chamber like an invading army. Lequeux was beginning seriously to doubt the wisdom of his move. Then the elders came; an interminable procession of limping, snuffling, coughing, swag-bellied old dotards. Lequeux heaved a sigh of relief. He had long experience of aged men and knew that fundamentally they all had the same way of thinking. He also knew a good deal about their passion for deliberation, or, to put it less politely, their passivity and sloth.

It took the French officials two full hours to find their way through this incredible jungle of local custom and tradition and unravel the quarrel between native shibboleth and Christian doctrine. Two hours of patient interrogation, muddled work by the interpreters and passionate disputes. The true nature of the affair was soon revealed to Lequeux and his associates. After a good deal of reticence and hesitation, the young Ebibot tribesmen accused one White man in the presence of another. Once they had taken this plunge, their complaints poured out unendingly. They made Le Guen their general scapegoat, saddling him with the responsibility for everything that had gone wrong. Little by little they became bolder in their attitude. Eventually they went so far as to demand Le Guen's removal. Throughout this diatribe there was a certain marked consistency about their observations which did not fail to strike Lequeux. The Administrator was gradually forming his own private theory concerning the quarrel and deciding what steps he would take when the time came.

When he had completed his interrogation of the young men, Lequeux turned his attention to the Elders. Addressing them in their double capacity as spiritual mentors and guardians of tribal tradition, he asked their opinion of this grave incident. His hope that they would condemn the missionary in even stronger terms than their juniors had done was rudely disappointed. To his surprise, they answered that they had no definite opinions and could not produce arguments in support of their position. Even old Yosifa, who might have been expected to prove a serious, persistent exponent of the Christian viewpoint, declared that though the Chief might be free to embrace the Catholic religion—including monogamy, if he felt inclined—his former wives could not be evicted from Essazam. Still less could they be turned out of the Ebazok clan. Their marriages to the Chief had made them life-members. In any case the tribe had no intention of honouring this act of repudiation.

Such a proposal preserved, virtually intact. the spirit of contradiction which Le Guen refused to leave unresolved. This time Lequeux was himself the victim of that goat-and-cabbage mentality, as it might be termed. Formerly he had found it an attractive feature of the Bantu. The elders of those tribes among which his career had been spent possessed the quality to a marked degree. In order to give himself a decent interval to think the matter over and also possibly to consult with certain friends in Ongola, he announced that he would hold a grand palaver in Essazam on the following Sunday. As many members of the tribe as possible should attend. He had forgotten the punishments which he had originally intended imposing on the riotous young men. His sole interest now was in the conflict between Le Guen, the missionary, and the whole Essazam confederacy. This formed an extremely large and important part of the area under his official jurisdiction.

When the French officials and their subordinates were about to take their leave, a rather odd-looking man made his way towards them. He wore a moth-eaten khaki drill uniform, with some military decoration or other pinned on his breast, and was energetically pushing through the crowd that crammed the audience-chamber. When he reached Lequeux he came smartly to attention, clicking his heels loudly. He was wearing an incredibly ancient pair of ammunition-boots. Then he presented himself, rather as a soldier might to his superior officer, reeling off his name, rank, and regiment; the arm in which he had served, the citations he had won, the considerable time he had spent on active service. He did not, of course, forget to mention that he had been present at that heroic undertaking, the capture of Kufra. Despite his rudimentary knowledge of French, he managed to make himself understood.

Carefully Raphael worked round to various platonic

edicts which the Administration had enforced several years earlier—in particular, one dealing with illicit distilling. He complained that this decree had been coolly and flagrantly broken by a certain young man who, because he fancied himself educated, had decided that he no longer need obey the law of the land. The Hero of Kufra went further. If the whole country was going to the dogs, he declared, the responsibility lay squarely on all these feather-brained city boys. They cared for nobody and nothing.

"Spivs, drunkards, deadbeat good-for-nothings the lot of them!"

As Lequeux made no move to stop this recital, Raphael plunged on. For weeks now, he alleged, this fellow had spent his time distilling extremely potent alcohol and selling it at exorbitant prices. The young people who had become involved in the regrettable brawl that afternoon had all imbibed large quantities of the hell-brew in question. At this point Lequeux asked Raphael various questions, which were answered smoothly enough. Raphael escaped the biggest risk he ran in denouncing Chris. This was that someone might recall his having taken a very active part himself in the riotous drinking session just described. In fact the party had been in the hut of Chris's aunt, shortly before the great fight broke out.

Lequeux thereupon made the Hero of Kufra take him to the hut in question. They stepped out, complete with escort. The official entourage trailed along behind. Inside the hut Chris, who really should have been more on his guard at this juncture, was busy with his interrupted distilling. He whistled happily as he worked. He did not even notice the tramp-tramp of the escort's boots outside. It was only his aunt's alarmed outcry which brought him to his senses and made him snap into action. When he moved, his presence of mind was astonishing. In his aunt's hut was a locked door opening directly on to the bush at the back, away from the village. Without hesitation Chris hurled himself at it, shoulder first. The door flew to bits under the impact. The wood had begun to rot as a result of damp and was not of particularly good quality anyway.

Chris found no difficulty in passing through the somewhat lax patrol-lines set up round the village. He plunged into the bush and quickly reached the shelter of the nearby jungle. From here he made his way to the river and hid himself in a large bush close to the bank. He held his breath and listened; nothing stirred. The native troops did not chase him far, or for any length of time.

Lequeux, who was conscious how futile such an operation would be in dense jungle, soon called off the search. Since he had no wish to persecute Chris's aunt, who was, after all, one of the Chief's wives, he announced that the charge would be dropped on condition that this young ruffian did not return to Essazam. If he *did* return, however, the native guards were under strict orders to apprehend him. Chris took great care to avoid giving them this pleasure.

"You see," Lequeux told Palmieri afterwards, chuckling triumphantly, "you see, M. Palmieri, I *really* know this little lot of mine. I was damn certain I could smell something pretty dirty in the wind."

Although it was by now very late in the evening, Lequeux insisted on going round to the Mission. He said he had one last word to say to Le Guen.

He found the priest still in bed.

"Well, Father, I'm afraid I'm here bothering you again. I'm so sorry, but it really is a matter of some urgency."

"There's no need to apologise," Le Guen said.

"I've just been having a long discussion with the villagers. Have you any idea how strong the popular feeling against you is? To think that you believe you're one

160

of them! In their eyes you're nothing but a stranger, a foreigner. Do you understand?"

Le Guen gave a thin smile. "That is by no means unlikely," he murmured.

"I must warn you, Father, that I shall not hesitate to use the full responsibility and power delegated to me in settling this affair—even with regard to yourself."

"You speak of—of action against *me*. May I enquire why?"

"It's merely a way of telling you that in apportioning praise or blame in this business I intend to stick rigorously to the letter of the law. My severity will take no account of private considerations or distinction between persons."

"I assure you, I am delighted to hear it. More than delighted," Le Guen said dryly.

"I am leaving a small detachment here, under the command of a French sergeant, to see that law and order are maintained. Also to prevent any further outbreak of trouble."

"Excellent, excellent!"

"And next Sunday we'll have it all thrashed out in public."

"We have plenty of spare beds here," Schloegel put in, with his usual conciliatory zeal. "Perhaps you would care——?"

"No thank you, really," Lequeux said. "It's absolutely essential for me to be back in Ongola by dawn tomorrow morning. We've got plenty on hand back there. Thank you again, though."

The first Sunday of September, 1948, lived up to expectations. It produced a fine crop of events. Though these may have lacked drama, they remained significant. The official party, Europeans and Africans alike, reached Essazam at an early hour. Immediately Lequeux set about "doing his duty". He began by inspecting the platoon which had been left behind in the village. The parade was a full-dress affair, its grandiose and colourful display calculated to inspire in the assembled populace admiration and respect for the authorities. It took place in the middle of the big square, which might have been made for such a purpose.

Finally the troops marched off. Only members of the tribe were left. These now gathered in a huge half-circle round the Chief and Lequeux. Some were sitting on folding chairs, the majority squatting in the dust. The official party also contained various government servants, African and European, together with the two Essazam missionaries. All these important personages had front-row seats. No audience-chamber would have been large enough for such a vast crowd. The honour of opening the proceedings fell to Ndibidi. With the sun already uncomfortably hot, he set about providing a choice sample of local eloquence.

The old man stood facing that sea of black faces. In order to protect themselves against the heat, no doubt, the Europeans felt constrained to lower their bandannas over their eyes at this point. Ndibidi strode to and fro, nostrils quivering, furiously thumping the ground with the butt-end of his spear. There was a positively haggard look in his eyes. He had to get his breath back after every two or three words. He interspersed each phrase, each aphorism, with inarticulate, drawn-out, unhappy exclamations. He would suddenly dart right across the square in a flash and come to an abrupt halt. After this he would touch his toes, straighten up again, beat his chest and pull back his shoulders. This little ceremony over, he came to the assembled tribesmen and put the finger on one of them—generally without saying a word by effectively staring his victim up and down in silence for several seconds. This done, he would resume his frantic gallop across the square, with the scarlet pom-pom on his bonnet fluttering behind him, its cord more blindingly green then ever.

Years later, when he was living in Europe, Bitama recalled this farcical performance and was surprised to see the similarity underlying all pretence, hypocrisy, and spiritual nihilism. Always strength was drawn from affected ritual, ceremonial face-pulling and organised waste of time.

The palaver, which an interpreter translated for the benefit of the Chief Regional Administrator as it proceeded, failed to take the affair a single step farther. It was, however, enlivened from time to time by various interventions; some aroused appreciative applause. This did not apply to Ondoua, whose irrelevant performance had nothing to do with the tribal conflict whatsoever. It was simply designed to obliterate the memory of Ndibidi from the minds of his audience.

Ondoua was followed by old Yosifa, who made a moving tribute to Anaba. This young girl, Yosifa said, had treated her with great generosity. Because of some detestable brawl Anaba had suffered nothing but pain in return for all her piety, her devotion to the sacred cause of old age. Modern youth as a whole treated this with such scant respect. Yosifa passed on to a lengthy lament about her own unhappy lot, calling the tribe to bear witness that misfortune had never failed to dog any wife of the Chief's who had wished her well. She who was his mother! And so on.

Mekanda, still terribly weak as a result of the wounds which Cecilia had inflicted on him, had himself carried on to the square. Ignoring the ostensible reason for the meeting, he announced to the assembled tribe his intention of marrying a young Essazam girl from the Ekabmeyong clan. What caused the real sensation was not so much the disclosure of his *fiancée's* identity (she was none other than young Medzo) but the revelation, by this brother of the Chief himself, that he, too, had been firmly converted to the Christian faith. He was determined to marry the girl in church at Essazam. Mekanda's pronouncement was greeted enthusiastically by the assembled company. The Chief, Lazarus Essomba as he now was, looked astonished and enraptured. He expressed a lively desire to see the girl who was to become his sister-in-law twice over and whom he only recalled as a small child. So Medzo stepped out in front of them all; missionaries, colonial officials, the whole tribe of the Essazam people.

She nervously moved her liquorice-coloured lips up and down, feeling for a tooth-pick which had wedged itself between her gleaming teeth. She was wearing a fixed smile, a kind of agonised grimace which made her look as though she were about to burst into tears. Perhaps she was. The presence of the Europeans and all these other strangers seemed to intimidate her. This constraint was offset by all sorts of instinctive tricks, half-animal, half-human. She wriggled her buttocks up and down, exactly like a mare about to pass wind. She shrugged her shoulders with the fluttering motion of a hen spreading its wings in a dust-bath. She indulged in an elementary, hip-wriggling coquetry.

As she passed by, the men whistled in admiration, or sniggered suggestively as people did when they saw two dogs copulating. Some of them, who knew her temperament, wondered whether Mekanda, who was a quiet, well-ordered sort of person, was not making a serious mistake in marrying such a she-devil. The women, who wrongly supposed her to have had a long, varied experience of intimacy with the male sex, asked one another how it was she had never had any children. They cast aspersions upon her fertility and quizzed her without mercy.

"Come here, child," the Chief said to her. Medzo obeyed. She curtsied deeply and, turning, offered the ecstatic crowd a full view of her incredible backside, which was the most irresistible feature about her.

After this the assembly could really savour the spectacle which Makrita presented. She was the very goddess of scrawniness, misery incarnated, a sad contrast to the lithe youthfulness and stunning beauty of the gorgeous animal who had preceded her. An old crone she was indeed, with scarcely more flesh on her bones than poor Yosifa. She was built like a man, flat-chested with a raddled face in which the eyes smouldered like those of a wounded tigress. Hatred flowed from the mouth of this frenzied virago like molten lava. She cursed and blasted away at them, consigning to perdition almost the entire population of Essazam. To listen to her, one would have thought every single person present had gone out of his way to do her harm. For hours, or so it seemed, she defied the traditional frailty of her sex, triumphantly trotting out her anathemas as though telling her beads.

To round off her speech she declared that Essazam was her home and expressed a lively desire to be told—in the presence of them all—just which man or woman it was had first dared discuss the matter of her departure. Or rather of her *eviction*. Next she moved across to Le Guen, who flushed up and looked rather uncomfortable at this attention to him. She took up a jaunty stance in front of the priest, hands on hips, left eye shut, and addressed him in challenging terms :

"Well, Father, nothing to say? I did hear a rumour, you know, that *you* were hoping I might leave the village. What's come over you all of a sudden? It wouldn't be that you haven't the guts to say what you think in public, would it?"

Le Guen said nothing and the old woman gave a loud, sarcastic laugh, rocking back and forth several times on her heels. When she had calmed down a little, she announced that she had no more to say. As far as she was concerned the matter would rest there. She was now going back to her house, as she felt somewhat tired.

It was then about two o'clock in the afternoon. The European contingent went off to the Catholic Mission for lunch. When they returned to the village to resume the palaver, they found the Essazam cheerful. They too had eaten and drunk well. All they would discuss now was a reconciliation. This in sharp contrast to Lequeux, still hunting for culprits. As was to be expected the Essazam point of view prevailed. The sleight-of-hand was worked in this way. It was a model performance in its class.

On the resumption, Maurice and Cecilia were brought before the assembly to face the charge of having attempted to murder their uncle. This was a little detail which had been carefully hidden from Lequeux till now. It was feared that he might take charge of the whole business and deprive the elders of what promised to be a most enjoyable entertainment.

The charges were read aloud by a kind of high priest, a grey skeleton of a ghostly old dotard who looked as though he had been specially exhumed to perform this task. He took some time over his performance, but put little conviction into it. He pronounced them guilty; stained with the blood of their "father"; threatened— unless they repented and changed their ways—with the everlasting curse of the gods. He promised them premature death, sterility, leprosy and other such unpleasant things by which their foul contagion would make itself known. He undertook to advise them how best to purify themselves. They would beg their "father" (that was, of course, their uncle) to forgive them in a form of public ceremony. They would bring on this occasion ten sheep for sacrifice. They would plunge their hands and forearms several times into the blood of these sheep and repeat a certain prayer for purification.

The pronouncement of this sentence evoked thunderous

applause among the tribal patriarchs. In accordance with custom, they would officiate at this expiatory ritual and gain the best share of the slaughtered sheep. Maurice and Cecilia, who had been informed earlier that it would be enough for them to accept the ceremony of purification in principle—their father, the Chief, was to supply the sheep—submitted to judgment with expressions of complete innocence. This little act sufficed to persuade those hoary councillors to support their mother's case. Mekanda's marriage and the purification of Maurice and Cecilia were both fixed for the following Sunday.

Though it was still long before sunset, the palaver was suddenly declared finished. The patriarchs affected to have hurried it to a close out of consideration for their White guests, whose delicacy of physique and propensity to sunstroke were well known. They declared themselves overwhelmingly grateful to the Europeans for having deigned to honour them with a visit, completely ignoring the fact that these colonial officials had only come to find out the truth about a highly serious incident. Caught off his guard and somewhat dazed both by the hot sun and the numerous speeches he had heard, Lequeux remained furious at having allowed himself to throw the game away in this fashion. When he set about the ceremonial business of shaking hands with the Elders, each whispered a few words in his ear, with sidelong glances at Le Guen. The latter had other fish to fry. In any case he was not particularly anxious to join in the leave-taking between Lequeux and his stalwart old gaffers.

"Tell your brother to leave our Chief in peace," they all hissed. "Why did he have to put it into the Chief's head to become a convert, eh, tell me that? Our fathers got on well enough without all that rubbish. The women will stay where they are, anyway. How could they go? Where would they go to? You tell him to leave the Chief alone! He can have the children and initiate them into his practices to his heart's content. We don't mind turning the children over to him, but he's got to keep his hands off the Chief. He's breaking up our peaceful existence, he's disturbing our traditions——"

Lequeux nodded, smiled condescendingly and promised to take action on such wise counsel.

Before they left, the European officials felt it incumbent upon them to honour the dinner-invitation from Le Guen. Also present was the African doctor, who had now become one of Le Guen's closest friends. Indeed, his affection for Essazam and its inhabitants seemed to have grown to such an extent that he never left the village at all. It was rather a tight squeeze to fit everyone into the dining-room of the Mission House, but Gustave and his friend the cook had gained some useful experience earlier in the afternoon in how to deal with this select yet unwieldy company.

Lequeux remained distrait for much of the meal. He looked both stern and care-worn. Giovanni Palmieri and his wife maintained their never-ending honeymoon. They were always looking deep into each other's eyes, smiling, even kissing from time to time, quite indifferent to the embarrassment which their behaviour was causing to their fellow-guests. This embarrassment aroused varying reactions. Schloegel, both in order to ease the atmosphere and distract attention from the loving couple, pumped out a stream of rather flat witticisms. Le Guen tried to show appreciation of this by laughing rather more loudly than usual. The doctor, whose sense of humour was severely limited, kept a fixed smile on his lips.

Nevertheless it was Giovanni Palmieri who, suddenly tiring of his amorous chit-chat, brought the conversation to life again. He gave it an intellectual turn which later produced a certain amount of friction.

"Father," the young Civil Servant said, addressing Le

Guen, "if I understand aright, your Chief is well-loved in his tribe, isn't he?"

" 'Adored' would be a more exact description," Le Guen asserted.

"Then it's out of the question that the tribe as a whole could wish him any harm?"

"Absolutely out of the question, M. Palmieri."

"In that case, don't you find it surprising that they left him to die—indeed, more or less abandoned him to rot in his corner?"

"Come, come," said Lequeux, with heavy irony. "Left him to rot, did they? That's the first I've heard of it."

"It's simply my way of expressing myself," Palmieri said. "Just a turn of phrase."

"Oh dear," Schloegel said, despondently. "Educated, too." Privately it struck him that for all his pedantry, the young man had a singularly ill-bred manner.

"Very well, then," Palmieri resumed. "They left him to die. What I mean is, no one thought of taking him to hospital."

"Listen, young man," Schloegel said, in the accent of weary experience. "If they don't believe in hospitals, what are we expected to do about it?"

"That's true enough," the doctor put in. "That they don't believe in hospitals, I mean."

"I find that very surprising," Palmieri persisted, stubbornly, conscious of his wife's adoring gaze. "Very surprising indeed. Tell me, er, ah——"

He floundered, in some embarrassment. He did not know the medical officer's name. Besides, since the fellow was not a proper doctor (as he put it to himself) he wondered whether it might not be tactless to address him as such. Finally, however, he decided to do so.

"Doctor, when you arrived in this village, you had free access to the house where the Chief was lying, did you not?"

"Certainly I did."

"No one tried to hinder you in the execution of your duties?"

"Nobody."

"Listen," Lequeux interrupted rudely. "Listen to me, M. Palmieri. I see exactly what you're driving at and I think you're wholly wrong. The doctor said they *didn't believe* in hospitals. He never claimed they were actively hostile to them."

"That's quite right," the doctor chimed in, like an echo. "I never claimed they were hostile to them. Besides, I'm an old friend of theirs, quite apart from the fact that obstructing a doctor in the execution of his professional duties is an offence which carries a quite heavy penalty."

And having thus put his foot in it he gave a cheerful belly-laugh.

"What do *you* think about it, Father?" said Palmieri, turning now to Le Guen.

"Well," said the priest, who had remained silent hitherto, "it's a highly complex problem, you see. I've known them half-kill themselves with overwork just to make enough money to take them to an American hospital some way from here: a good deal farther than Ongola. This leads me to a point I made to *Monsieur le Chef de la région* the other day. It irritated him and perhaps it will shock you. The truth of the matter is, what they lack is not so much faith in European medicine as in the hospital service at Ongola. The Americans, as we know, have only one hospital in the whole country. But look how well-equipped it is and how up-to-date the people there are!"

"Well then," Palmieri persisted, "why didn't they take him all the way to the American hospital?"

"Do you mind waiting a moment?" Le Guen said. He went out of the room and presently came back followed by Gustave. The boy looked at the tableful of grown-ups with wide and questioning eyes.

"Come here, Gustave," Le Guen said, sitting down again.

The boy moved towards him, but without any of that obsequious haste customary among young boys in those parts. He walked with a sedate, unhurried gait, easily and calmly. This somehow gave Lequeux the impression that the boy was intimidated.

"Don't be afraid, laddie," he said. "Come on, now, don't be so scared."

"Gustave," said Le Guen, with a faint smile, "listen carefully and think well before you answer."

"Are you quite sure he understands?" Lequeux asked.

"Why are you so convinced he doesn't?" Le Guen retorted cheerfully. "Now, tell me, Gustave: you've often been down in the village while the Chief was ill, haven't you?"

"Yes, Father," the boy said.

"And you kept your eyes open, didn't you? I'm sure you must have remembered a great deal of what you saw. For instance, was the Chief well looked after during his illness? Tell us a little about it. What sort of attention did he have and who gave it him?"

The boy went on for some time about the number of famous doctors and healers who had come to the Chief's bedside one after the other. He also gave details of the treatment each of them had prescribed—insomuch as a lay observer could understand it. From the boy's evidence it would appear that the tribe had done all that was humanly possible to save the Chief's life. They had not even hesitated to bring in top specialists, of their own free will incurring what, in such a case, was always an extremely heavy fee. As the boy spoke in French, Le Guen had no need to translate.

"Well?" he asked the others.

"He's a most extraordinary child," Mme Palmieri declared, enraptured. "*Most* extraordinary."

All the men laughed. Palmieri said to the boy: "Gustave, did anyone ever mention the idea of taking the invalid to hospital? Not even once?"

"No, Monsieur," said the boy, without hesitation.

"Don't answer the gentleman like that, Gustave," Le Guen said, with some severity. "Make an effort, child. Think. Try to remember. It's possible that such a suggestion was in fact made. Perhaps the people who made it were put off by the absence of any adequate transport, or by the dangerous condition of the patient, I don't know. Think carefully, Gustave. Well?"

The boy had lowered his eyes while he searched his memory; now he raised them again, looked Le Guen straight in the face and shook his head.

"No," he whispered. "I don't remember hearing anyone mention such a thing, not even once."

"No? Not even once? Are you sure?"

"Quite sure, Father."

"Very well. You can go to bed now."

Scarcely was Gustave out of the room than Le Guen went on to the rest of them: "There you are! The facts aren't in doubt. There was never any question of the Chief being taken to hospital. If my boy says not, that's how it was."

Lequeux said, sarcastically: "Yet every single person who passes for a man of wisdom in this tribe was right on the spot. And, as the boy has just told us, there came a moment when the traditional healers and medicine-men gave up hope and felt they could do no more. Even so, it did not occur to any of them that the patient's life might be saved if he were taken to hospital. Well, M. Palmieri, will you perhaps one day supply us with the key to this incredible behaviour? How would it be explained by a sociologist?"

Palmieri began by pulling a face, the kind of self-depre-cating grin which academics affect when forced to ex-plain themselves to the vulgar herd. The Great Brain himself, with modesty only exceeded by erudition, never completely discarded the possibility of error.

"Well," he said at last, the grin still hovering on his lips, "there is nothing, when all's said and done, you know, to suggest that what we have experienced is other than an exceedingly commonplace phenomenon of human de-velopment."

"Oh yes?" said Lequeux, "and what might this com-monplace phenomenon be?"

"At a certain stage of their evolution a people will retain the illusion of activity, decision, initiative. In fact their nature has changed in such a way that they can do nothing except endure passively whatever may befall them."

"And you call that a stage in their evolution?" Lequeux said, pugnaciously. "A stage in their decadence, you mean."

"In sociology," Palmieri continued patiently, "the idea of 'development' is rather like that of an equation. As we all know, any statement in algebra can be preceded by either a plus or a minus sign——"

"Well, that's one thing we're agreed on," chortled Lequeux, raising his hands in mock-applause.

"If you say so," Palmieri sighed. "Still, I don't like the term 'decadence'. It's not scientific; it carries an implied value-judgment, and presupposes an ethical system."

"I have a most important piece of news to tell you," Lequeux said smoothly, turning to his host. "I am leaving Monsieur Giovanni Palmieri here among you. A decision has been taken, at the highest level, to form a new ad-ministrative district. Its headquarters will be here at Essazam. Right on top of you! You were a little, ah, *under-administered*, it was felt. Well, Father, do you know who will be the new district's first Administrative Officer? Monsieur Giovanni Palmieri! You are under his jurisdiction as from this very moment. For once M. Palmieri will have real problems on which to exercise his talents—concrete problems. That ought to do him good, don't you think, Father? He'll have to start the whole thing from scratch. You'll soon find out, Palmieri, that an administrator hasn't always time to be a philosopher as well."

"I'm sure things will turn out very well indeed," Le Guen said to Palmieri, with the ghost of a wink.

Palmieri sat there in some confusion, sucking nervously at his pipe, while his wife, her eyes still fixed on his face, now gave him a swooningly tender smile. In any other woman such a gesture would have seemed more exaggerated than it did on this occasion. Madame Palmieri still looked like a schoolgirl.

"Ah yes!" sighed Lequeux. "I hope he brings it off, too; but I advise him not to indulge in any illusions. A colonial administrator isn't such a glamorous chap in 1948. It doesn't matter how many puddles or potholes there are in the road. You can still get into town in a matter of hours with a jeep. All the same, you won't be short of willing helpers, with the number of young fellows getting their school certificate these days—and God knows what else in the process. You'll hardly need even an interpreter, to judge by what we just heard from Gustave. I know some provinces in France where the young children don't get the chance to speak as clearly and well as he does. But Gustave is exactly what I'm afraid of, you know, Palmieri. Yes indeed: the Gustaves will be your problem. I'm afraid they will make life very difficult for you. Infinitely harder and more difficult than it ever was for me."

"If it only were a matter of the Gustaves!" Palmieri said, half to himself. "I'm thinking of a very different character, who's probably lying in wait for me down the

174

road at this very minute. You know, the fellow we caught distilling alcohol the other day, who got away into the jungle."

"Oho," said Lequeux bitterly, "indeed yes. We'll see who was right about him one day, we will indeed."

"Is it really essential to prove oneself right?" Le Guen asked, his eyes fixed on the ceiling.

"Look, old boy," said Schloegel suddenly to the doctor, "do you think that young girl will pull through all right?"

"Oh yes, no doubt about it. She'll recover very easily; it'll hardly leave a scratch on her."

The conversation stopped when the cook came in to clear the plates away and resumed as soon as he was out of the room.

"That girl's like all the women in this country," the doctor said. "Built like a mare."

"Why not like an antelope?" asked Schloegel, who loved working in bits of local colour.

"What exactly happened, old boy?" Le Guen asked. "You were down in the village. How on earth could those women bring themselves to manhandle her so badly that she had a miscarriage?"

"You know," the doctor began, and then shook his head as Le Guen offered him a cup of coffee. "No thanks: I never touch the stuff. Now, what was I saying? Oh yes. The truth of the matter is that I wasn't really there when all this was happening. I was some way from the spot. The thing is, it all depends upon the woman. Sometimes even the slightest little shock will do the trick—something quite negligible. As far as I've been able to make out— the evidence was very confused, you know—this girl slipped and fell. The other women tumbled over her while they were fighting among themselves."

"But *why*?" Schloegel demanded. "Why did they do a thing like that? Surely there must be a reason? Perhaps

175

they bore her a grudge because she was the one the Chief had elected to be his only wife?"

Lequeux sniggered. "I must say, 'elected' is pitching it a bit high, don't you think?"

"This is the kind of mentality which it's quite impossible for you to understand," the doctor explained, in all seriousness. "We have to face such problems, but I'm well aware that they don't extend to people of your race and temperament. I know. I spent part of the last war in Europe. I know a woman who lives quite near Ongola. One day she was caught in the act of stealing a stem of maize from her neighbour's field. Nothing of any value, you see. And I have no doubt her neighbour would gladly have given it her, if she'd asked for it. But instead of asking for it, she took it upon herself to steal it and was caught. As soon as the story spread about, dozens of cruel little lampoons were made up about it. For this poor light-fingered creature every word in those lampoons struck home like a poisoned arrow. And that wasn't the end of it. The wretched woman didn't have anywhere to go and hide. So one day, unable to stand it all any longer——"

"Surely she didn't kill herself?" Schloegel interjected.

"Not exactly; but what she did was almost the same thing. She went away, left home. You see, the other clans all felt horribly insulted when the Chief—ah—elected this girl, or perhaps I should say, this lady. Afterwards the merest allusion would be enough to——"

"Do men suffer from this particular kind of touchiness, too?"

"Well, there's a male equivalent."

"But look," Schloegel went on, bringing all his heavy peasant commonsense to bear on the problem. "Let's take your case, my friend. You've gone through some pretty tough professional hoops, haven't you? Don't tell me you feel the same way." Schloegel was beyond doubt a native of the Rhine Valley.

"Personally," the doctor said, "I've always given way in the face of brute strength. I never see any point in fighting."

"But all the same——" Schloegel muttered.

"Listen! I had a girl-friend once—not half a gorgeous bit she was, too." The doctor, very much at his ease after several glasses of wine, was now talking with a noticeable accent, straight out of the Ongola back-streets. "Well, I was taking a stroll through an out-of-the-way part of the city and what do I see there? A bloody big young chap, standing there like *so*. He gets right in front of me and stays there, blocking my path, *so*. Fair enough, I step aside to avoid him. *But* he repeats his little dodge all over again. This time I saw him coming. I know his sort. Have to. After a bit more of it, he saw I wasn't going to be fool enough to lose my temper. So *then* he makes up his mind to speak to me. 'Christ,' he says. 'look at this thing here. Hasn't even got what it takes and it thinks it can muck about with real men.' So I say to him, 'Look, old boy, what's your trouble?' 'Oh,' he says, 'smart bugger, too, eh? Well, get this straight: you speak one more word to Jacqueline and see what happens to you. I'll roast you alive, do you hear? Like a bloody baa-lamb.'"

"And what did you say to that?" enquired Lequeux, who was enjoying this more than anyone.

"Well, *then* I promised him I'd never speak to Jacqueline again and that was the end of it," said the doctor, ingenuously.

"In more civilised countries," said Palmieri, who was a very high-flying sort of humanist, "it is, perhaps, true that people don't half-kill each other any more for such base motives. But it's not very long since much less than that would have caused a duel, even in Europe. It's Humanity as a whole that refuses to develop as it should. We all have our wretched little individual pride somewhere. In the Middle Ages it called itself chivalry. Later it disguised itself as a sense of honour. In our day dignity is all the rage."

"In Viet-Nam their attitude is very similar to here," Lequeux remarked. "They're just as absurdly touchy and cut one another to bits for equally futile reasons."

"You've been in Viet-Nam, have you?" Le Guen enquired, admiringly.

"Have I been to Viet-Nam!" Lequeux chortled. "My dear Father Le Guen, I was born there. I am half Viet-Namese myself. My mother was a pure-bred native woman. Only my father was French—or White, if you prefer it. I know the Viet-Namese exceedingly well, better than the Negroes, even. Yes, Father: I've seen all shades of colour in my time, as I've told you. All sorts and conditions."

Sensing that the two men were determined to have it out together and fairly soon at that, Schloegel rose. The doctor, Palmieri and Palmieri's wife followed suit. They all prepared to sally forth into the night. They decided to go back to the village and rout out one or two really picturesque old patriarchs.

"We'll leave you to it," Schloegel said to Lequeux and his fellow-priest. "Can't help feeling you want to have a little heart-to-heart chat. Well, enjoy yourselves! We're going to stroll down to the village and tease some of our eloquent local sages. *Sages*—I ask you——"

"Take care not to dawdle between the Mission and the village, Brother Joseph," Le Guen said, with a faint but perceptible sternness of tone in his voice. He pointed out into the night, now growing darker still as a storm blew up on the distant horizon. "It's nearly a mile, maybe more, between here and the village. I'm thinking especially of Mme Palmieri; she shouldn't be needlessly exposed to the elements."

Still reassuring Le Guen, they all four stepped shoulder to shoulder into the darkness. Already the wind was rising.

rustling through the trees, filling the whole forest with a kind of vibrant humming sound.

"Well, Father, let's have your verdict on this affair," Lequeux said, tapping a cigarette on the back of his hand.

"What affair, might I enquire?" Le Guen said, in all innocence.

"What? Why, the affair of—what would you call it? This conversion, eh? *Conversion.* H'm."

"With all due respect, *Monsieur le Chef de la région,* there is no affair. There is no affair. Consequently I have no verdict upon it."

"So that's your line, is it? Come now, Father, be serious. They are solidly united against you, absolutely, I might say. Haven't you even noticed?"

"As far as I am concerned, that is not of the least importance. Christ too, in his day, ran up against a united opposition. Men never like being told to change their ways."

"And a very good thing too. Why do you want to change them, Father? They seem to me quite all right as they are."

"Ah! They seem to you quite all right as they are, do they?" Le Guen exclaimed. He had struggled to his feet and his nostrils quivered with rage.

"Father, I believe in God, but I don't believe in magic. Few people could say as much. What sort of wizard's wand are you going to wave to pluck one of these natives out of an instinctive tradition that's taken thousands of generations to evolve?"

"My wand will be God's Grace, *Monsieur le Chef de la région.*"

"Magic, just as I said. After all—— Come, Father, we must try and reach some agreement. I've got to be on my way from here in an hour's time at the very latest. I want you to swear solemnly to me, on your word of honour as a priest and a Frenchman, that you will in future abandon the crazy scheme of converting the Chief. I want you to renounce this scheme, without any second thoughts. Without the idea of ever coming back to it. Will you swear this to me?"

"Forgive me for saying this, Monsieur Lequeux, but I must tell you that you don't understand the first thing about this problem."

"I know, Father. I know I don't understand you; but equally I know that you don't understand me. Try and make some slight effort to—to put yourself in my place. Imagine, if you can, the very ordinary, prosaic responsibilities I have. Of the earth, earthy, most of them. Often requiring immediate decisions. Well, then, since they *are* my decisions, kindly leave them to me. For my part I gladly resign to you your cure of souls and concern with the future. To put it another way, the women and children. Proselytise them as much as you please—convert them, hear their confessions, make them saints in the Catholic calendar, if you feel like it. Nobody'll be a penny the worse. But when you interfere with the older generations, Father, you put us in an unbelievably embarrassing position. It's not very much that I'm asking you to leave me. Only the past, after all. Compare it with the future I'm bequeathing to you! We've already managed to convince a certain number of Fathers Superior in the Missions that our view of this delicate matter is the correct one. I've got used to dealing with such questions. One doesn't spend long years working in Africa and gain nothing. You aren't the first person I've had this argument with. But I think I can say you'll be the last—and with good reason.

"You see, you'd been represented to me as being quite unshakable. That's why I decided not to broach you in cold blood, as it were, but to await the crucial moment. I had my doubts as to whether you would ever reach that point on your own. The time has come today. You see,

Father, we live in troubled times—times in which it is vital that Africa should remain free of disturbances. Who can tell where the slightest agitation might lead us? The most important thing for all of us at the moment, Father —more important than the conversion of souls to God, more important than anything else—is surely the continuation of our presence here? Perhaps I should say the continuation of that peace which we both, in our own way, have succeeded in establishing among these disinherited people. Consider their brutish ignorance of good and evil. I'm certain you realise this, Father. Believe me— and I speak from a very long experience of colonial administration—one outbreak gives rise to another. This triggers off a third and so on to the next. What you get in the end is real subversion, Father. Come now! Won't you make me that little promise I'm asking you for?"

"NO!!"

"Take care what you are saying, Father. The only reason I've cooked up this bastard compromise solution I'm offering you is, quite simply, because you inspire me with affection and sympathy. I warn you, if you push me beyond the limit, I may be forced to resort to less friendly methods."

"I have said 'No' already. I will say it again: *NO!!!* What you ask of me is absolutely unthinkable. I would never accept such a proposal, even if it came from my Bishop himself. In any case, the problem is artificial."

"Really?"

"Absolutely, my dear Lequeux. It is impossible for me to promise, under oath, whoever seeks to make me do so, that I will turn my face away from a soul that is seeking the road to God and calling on me for help. The Chief is a free man. His choice will be freely made."

"Free, eh?" Lequeux exclaimed, with a vast guffaw "That's a good one! *Free!*"

And he laughed and laughed till he was out of breath.

Then, paler now, he fixed Le Guen with his fiercest, most angry expression and whispered: "When you get down to rock-bottom, what difference is there between you and any Communist agitator? Tell me that now. What's the difference between you and a Red? You are equally the evil genius of all peaceful, easy-going peoples—people who ask nothing better, believe you me, than to stay as they are. You never rest till you have stirred up these innocent, harmless people by inculcating dangerous, illusive notions. Things like Liberty and Equality before God, Redemption, Brotherhood and heaven knows what other twaddle. Why the hell can't you leave them in peace? It's all they ask."

Everything was banging about outside in the wind. Le Guen had to shut the two dining-room windows, struggling against the squalls like someone trying to push a small child inside a crowded bus. Presently he came back, sat down opposite Lequeux and said: "*Monsieur le Chef de la région*, I'm sorry, truly sorry to cause you so much trouble. But you see, my function is not to act as a guardian of slumbering humanity."

"You know, all the irresponsible fools in the world talk just like you. You're a child who gets some fun out of poking a sleeping snake; but very soon the snake will rouse itself and then what? I prefer not to think what will happen. Father, you should go and see something of what is happening in Indo-China at this very moment. A part of the world which would be nothing without the genius of France. It'd do you a great deal of good to go there for a few weeks. Believe me, you're a Sorcerer's Apprentice without knowing it. Before the Japanese invasion there was a comfortable peace all around us out there—just as there is here today. Frenchmen and Natives were fond of each other and respected one another. From the fertile union of the two strains many sweet fruits were produced. I ought to know: I'm one of them. I have, I think, already told you that my father was French and my mother Viet-

Namese. *Was*: past tense, unfortunately. A year ago some bloody-minded fanatics got into our house at Hanoi and murdered both of them. The cowardly swine! They were Reds, that goes without saying. And when did this happen? After the Japs had gone and everything was getting back to normal. And do you know where these criminal fanatics came from? From Christian mission-schools, as it happened. They were *Christians*, do you hear? *Christians*, as only you bloody missionaries know how to turn them out."

One moment he was blazingly angry, the next uttering heavy, drawn-out sighs of misery. He could change in an instant from the most furious temper to the depths of despair. Both conditions were induced by the same poison; one of those afflictions that alternately exasperate the patient into a frenzy and plunge him into lethargy. All the time he was hag-ridden by a kind of obsession that appeared to act on him like a truth-drug, forcing him to go on talking, pouring out incessant confidences.

"And who, I might ask, is our most ferocious and implacable enemy today? Why, the Tonkinese, of course. The Tonkinese for whom we've done so much. We gave them everything—even bishops. Since you seem to have a compulsive urge to make new Christians, Father, go ahead and make as many of them in this country as you like. But I warn you: for every Christian you'll soon have one more Red as well. What's more, when they start slitting throats, you'll be their first victim. It's inevitable. No one will ever convince me, *ever*, that Tonkin wasn't better off in the old days, when the peasant peacefully tilled his land, the fisherman sat by the river and the French Administration took care of them both. It was only when the Communists started meddling in their affairs that——"

"All this clap-trap doesn't interest me in the least," Le

Guen suddenly declared, with unpardonable rudeness, rising to his full height the better to outstare this poor little runt of a Lequeux. "I'm here at this moment, not in Viet-Nam. We simply don't speak the same language. All this stuff you're dinning into me just bores me to tears."

"Really, now. Does it? Very well, Father. We shall see. We shall see."

And they stood there face to face, without saying another word, till the rain stopped. Then Lequeux went out with a curt "Goodbye" and walked back to the village, where the Chief swore he would see to it that no more disturbances took place in Essazam. Nevertheless Lequeux decided to leave the guard-detachment where it was till the various clans had dispersed. Then, that same night, he left once more by jeep for Ongola.

"The great Satrap has just left me," Le Guen wrote to his mother. *"We had a really deadly quarrel and I shall be most surprised if he doesn't punish me for my insolence. Imagine, Mama, I told him to his face that all his clap-trap bored me stiff! He would persist in going on about Viet-Nam—tears and melodrama turn and turn about. It seems he was born there. He also tried to make me swear that I would give up my efforts to convert your Bantu monarch—your King Lazarus himself! The truth is, things aren't all going as they might in this part of the world. It's a complicated story, believe me. . . .*

". . . As you may surmise, there is an extreme degree of confusion here. My superiors in the Hierarchy are putting pressure on me to, as it were, accelerate, while my lord the Satrap insists that I should apply the brakes. So you see . . .

"To go back to the state of confusion which reigns here, it seems that no one is free of it. I couldn't begin to tell you, dear Mama, exactly what my own position is now. I went to a great deal of trouble to make innovations, to

leave the well-beaten track, to steer clear of the easy com-
promises which everyone here, as far as I can see, is only
too ready to adopt. But at the moment I am very far from
congratulating myself. After all, since baptism leaves an
indelible mark, surely my duty is, quite simply, to lay my
hands on as many converts as I may and stop tormenting
myself with all sorts of considerations which have really
nothing to do with my missionary work here? To think
of all the reservations I have been making these past ten
years about Reverend Father Drumont! I console myself
by repeating the old tag about fools never changing—or
so they say. . . .

". . . The Satrap will undoubtedly have a little decision
to take on my account. From what I have heard and what
he has told me himself in his official capacity, he has not
the slightest intention of putting himself in the wrong or
admitting that the blame lies with him. What is worrying
me is how the Hierarchy will react. Is it too presumptuous
of me to hope that they will continue to give me their
backing and support? . . ."

Schloegel, together with the Palmieris, was back very
late at the Mission and found Le Guen just finishing his
long letter to his mother.

"Your medical chum sends you all manner of courteous
greetings, Your Reverence," Brother Joseph told his colleague. "He's sleeping in the Chief's apartments. How did
things go off with our Administrator-in-Chief, Head of the
Region, etcetera, etcetera? Well, I hope?"

"Oh yes," Le Guen told him, with amiable good humour.
"We finally had an open row."

"I'm forced to admit that it must be very difficult indeed *not* to have open rows with our little friend,"
Palmieri declared, sure now of being approved.

"Ah yes," Schloegel observed. "In your position, such
as it is, I've no doubt you've frequently given His Nibs

a piece of your mind. Shame on you, you ungrateful ink-slinger! You're a Bad Influence."

"Father," Palmieri said to Le Guen, "dealing with one's superiors is a hell of a problem, isn't it? I haven't been in this game very long, but I'm finding it an alarming business already."

"It all depends where you want to end up," Le Guen said, benevolently. "If you frequently dream of being a Colonial Governor, then you should be watching your step already. Otherwise it's all as easy as kiss-your-hand. There's one infallible method, as advocated by dear old La Fontaine: If a storm blows, become a reed—a small, very flexible reed. As soon as the storm is past, you can stand up straight once more. It's very simple."

"Thank you, Father," Palmieri said. "I've been spending these last few days regretting the fact that the Colonial Office, instead of teaching us the art of command, only instructs us how to think logically. Paris can produce nothing but hair-splitters, by the look of it."

"Don't lose your head, please. Just do what you think you ought to do, that's all."

"Yes, but one needs to be realistic, after all, Father," Palmieri said. "Sometimes the only positive argument one has is a bayonet."

"It doesn't matter; you must still have faith," Le Guen told him.

"Come, children," said Schloegel, gruffly. "Come and see your room. You can continue this interesting discussion tomorrow morning. His Reverence must get some sleep now. . . . Tell me, Your Reverence, do you suppose the Chief will invite them to live in his place till he's built a Residency? What do you think, Your Reverence?"

"Oh well, if he likes the idea, I suppose . . . What do you think, Monsieur—er——"

"Palmieri: Giovanni Palmieri. Really, I don't know——"

"You'll have plenty of time to think it over," Le Guen

186

said. "While you're making up your mind, you can stay in the Mission as long as you like."

"Come along now, you two turtle-doves," Schloegel said. "Come, come, come——"

Before they dispersed and not knowing that this would be the very last time that they ever hob-nobbed with Le Guen, the Essazam tribe celebrated—with much pomp and circumstance—a marriage in church between Robert Mekanda Mendouga and Laurentine Evina: Medzo, it turned out, was only a nickname.

The two young people, who had both been baptised the previous evening, were solemnly joined in the bonds of matrimony in the Catholic Church of Essazam, by the Abbé Joachim Eloumden, himself an Essazam of the Eyibone clan, whom Le Guen had asked to officiate in order to underline the symbolic significance of this day. Throughout the service Le 'Guen himself played rather grandiose Handel voluntaries on the new Mission harmonium. This music sent the Essazam into ecstasies— even the Elders, who had deigned to come to church in order to mark the happy event with the seal of their presence. Ondoua, and his inseparable companion Ndibidi, sat side by side whispering frequently to one another and chewing kola the whole time. The young Ebibots were remarkable for the irritating habit they had of scratching themselves like nervous monkeys.

When they came out of church, Brother Joseph appointed himself an impromptu official photographer. He took several shots of the patriarchs (the Grand Electors, as Palmieri called them) as they gathered round Le Guen. The priest himself took his place between the bride, who was attired in a frightful dress only redeemed by its immaculate white veil, and the happy bridegroom, heavily disguised in a ghastly reach-me-down suit.

Everyone was radiating cheerfulness. This marriage was

some sort of compensation for the Chief's. It pleased them by its ostentation, if not its Christian ritual. An immense feast now followed the wedding. All day long the village of Essazam was festooned with circles of women, all shimmying away gracefully, and young men whirling like dervishes to the rhythmic beat of the tom-toms. Palmieri and Bitama, who could hardly have failed to strike up an immediate and lasting friendship, wandered through the village together, stopping by each cluster of dancers, falling under the spell of the music, the singing, the rhythm and bright colours. As the sun sank on this festive day, Palmieri, who was with some difficulty fighting off a mood of sheer romantic ecstasy, said to his new friend: "Well, dear boy, I'm simply astounded at the extraordinary gaiety which marriage seems to provoke among your people. Today the Essazam made me think of every great civilisation the world has known—the Egyptians, the Greeks, the Romans, the Carthaginians and a score of others. They put me in mind of all those who, down the ages, have thus honoured the sacrifice which a young virgin is to make at nightfall for her lover. The sacrifice of her finest treasure. Isn't that a lovely thought? There's so much to be thankful for, don't you think?"

Bitama said, very simply: "I wouldn't like to be married that way."

"Why not, my friend?"

"I wouldn't like to bring so many people in on an affair which ought to concern no one except my bride and myself. It would seem unseemly to me."

That same week the tribe was dispersed to the four winds once more. The upcountry clans went back to their fields and forests; Essazam regained its usual somnolent calm and very soon the grave incidents were no more than a memory.

The Chief very quickly forgot not only his illness but

also his stray impulse towards conversion. He choked off even the proselytising fervour of Le Guen. The latter sadly saw the disagreement between himself and the Satrap taking an unfortunate turn. Essomba Mendouga, though he carried the additional burden of the name Lazarus, soon rediscovered the joys of polygamy and strict obedience to tribal ethics. Yet he never entirely lost the obsession that one day he would have to render an account of his life to God—a Mysterious Being, more powerful perhaps even than Akomo. And—who knew?—endowed with the thin lips and piercing blue eyes of his friend Le Guen.

Even years afterwards this obscure fear stirred him to panic whenever he felt in the least ill. On these occasions he would summon his wives, give them their freedom and insist on making his Confession so that he would be able to receive Communion and take his place in the Heavenly Feast among God's Elect, dressed in a white robe. The wives never troubled to leave home. As soon as the crisis was over, the Chief was only too glad to see them back again.

It was shortly before the end of 1948 that Le Guen received the following letter:

Ongola, 20th November 1948
From: The High Commissioner's Office of the French Republic.
To: The Reverend Father Jean-Marie Le Guen, Superior of the Catholic Mission in Essazam.

Dear Sir: We have the honour to inform you that there is now in our possession a detailed and circumstantial account of the regrettable incidents which, early in September of this year, brought you into conflict with Etienne-André Lequeux, Colonial Administrator-in-Chief and

189

Chief of the N—— region, under whose jurisdiction you are placed.

Though we regret the necessity of saying this, it appears from this circumstantial report that, notwithstanding the almost criminal position in which you quite deliberately had put yourself, i.e. by compelling (on moral grounds, it is true) a Tribal Chief to renounce his ancestral way of life, nevertheless your attitude when confronted by an official representative of the Republic did not convey that overall propriety and dignified friendliness which would hardly have been too much to expect in such circumstances, which we willingly admit were somewhat delicate.

Even though you have never, to our knowledge, been in ignorance of the fact, you will, we hope, reaffirm, as we do, the fundamental unity of the Mission for which together we have been made responsible by our dear motherland, France, in the midst of these savage peoples.

Even though you may never have questioned such a rule, we would like with your permission to remind you that this Mission, though it is, as we have said, a fundamental unity, nevertheless does embrace three essential aspects: theological, ideological, and—last but not least—administrative. The duty of realising each aspect, in the best interests of our subject peoples, falls upon three different types of men. . . .

How could we ever express to you the nobility of the rôle which had fallen to you? Which we esteemed more highly than you ever did yourself, praising your actions even though you could not hear us, ranging ourselves solidly behind you in your efforts!

How was it that you did not feel the same urgent need for this solidarity that we did? Why did you leave us to cultivate our relationship in so one-sided a fashion? Why did it have to be that at a time as decisive and pregnant with future history as this post-war era—an era fertile in foolish rebellions, revolts that prejudice the fame and glory of our great country, France—why did it have to be, we repeat, that your road should diverge so sharply and permanently from the objectives which we once had in common?

It is therefore we, be well assured of that, who, for the reasons we have outlined above (and which you will have no difficulty in understanding) have suggested to your ecclesiastical superiors your transfer from your present post. This they will no doubt inform you themselves in due course.

As in the past, we shall continue to stand firmly behind you and to consider your aims and ours as one. We trust that you will prove willing to return the compliment.

We are, Sir, you obedient and humble servants:

[There follow the signatures]:

The High Commissioner's Office of the French Republic.
For the Secretary-General of the High Commissioner's Office:
I. Destailles.

For the Secretary-General, the Colonial Office:
K. Schreiben.

Principal Private Secretary, for the Minister:
[signature illegible].